"Why did you have to disrupt my life?"

Dane's eyes glinted in the sun.

"I'm not disrupting anyone's life! I was stranded here—and I'm stuck here until I can get off."

"You seem content with the life of the islands, but how soon before you long for the excitement of the city, long for plays and nightclubs and parties?"

"Not me—you have me confused with the other women you hang out with." Mary-Kate leaned forward, her face only inches from Dane's. "I like a good time, but I wouldn't miss nightclubs. Friends are important to me, and I like staying home and visiting."

"It's easy to say that now, but how would you feel after several months here?"

"I won't be here that long, remember. I'm leaving on the supply boat when it comes."

"I remember! And it can't come too soon!" he replied harshly.

Barbara McMahon and her two daughters share their home in the San Francisco Bay area with one dog, two cats and pair of rabbits. Before settling down to work for a computer-software company, Barbara's stint as an airline stewardess took her all over the world. But her favorite place remains the Sierra Nevada where one day she hopes to live and write full-time.

Books by Barbara McMahon

HARLEQUIN ROMANCE
2643—COME INTO THE SUN
2777—BLUEBELLS ON THE HILL
2895—WINTER STRANGER, SUMMER LOVER

ISLAND PARADISE
Barbara McMahon

Harlequin Books

TORONTO • NEW YORK • LONDON
AMSTERDAM • PARIS • SYDNEY • HAMBURG
STOCKHOLM • ATHENS • TOKYO • MILAN
MADRID • WARSAW • BUDAPEST • AUCKLAND

Original hardcover edition published in 1992
by Mills & Boon Limited

ISBN 0-373-03221-8

Harlequin Romance first edition September 1992

ISLAND PARADISE

CHAPTER ONE

MARY-KATE was startled awake to the sounds of snarling dogs and male voices yelling. For an instant she froze, lying perfectly still, trying to figure out what was happening, where she was. Her heart pounded, her breathing was shallow. She was afraid to move. Was there danger near by?

The heat from the sun caressed her back; the fine white sand felt like talc beneath her fingers. She lifted her head slowly and surveyed the palm-fringed beach. Of course, she was sunbathing on a deserted beach on one of the small islands of Hawaii. But it was men's voices raised in anger that had disturbed the tranquil setting and woken her.

She heard a motor roar, and scrambled up, frantically reaching to refasten her bathing suit strap. She had untied the top so as to have no tan lines. Her fingers fumbled in her haste, and she dropped the string. Found it again.

The skimpy hot-pink bikini was not sold in Ames, Iowa. She had splurged on it in Honolulu when the boat had stopped there. Today was only the second time she'd worn it. She was too modest to wear it as casually as the bronzed women of Honolulu, but the deserted beach had seemed safe. She wanted a good tan, but was terribly self-conscious about the amount of skin the suit revealed. It would have been downright risqué in Iowa, but was the norm in Hawaii.

If her students could see her now, they'd be shocked. She smiled, remembering the feeling of recklessness that had engulfed her at the store in Honolulu. This was the most daring piece of clothing she'd ever purchased. She didn't know if it was because no one knew her here, or that the warm tropical air caused everyone to be more casual, but she was glad she'd bought the suit.

The yelling ended, but the dogs continued to bark; the sound of the motor gradually diminished. What was going on? Mary-Kate grabbed her towel and her short cotton wrap, thrusting her feet into her sandals. The others from the boat party had been around the jut of land that cut her off from them, in the direction of the noise. She had to find out what was happening.

Running was impossible. The sand gave beneath her every step, the hot, humid air was like a wall, hard to push through. Mary-Kate settled to a steady but quick pace, veering toward the water to walk on the firm, damp sand. It seemed to take ages to reach the other beach.

She heard another engine, quieter, also fading. Then nothing but silence and the soft lap of the ocean against the sand. Rounding the headland, she saw the other beach. Pristine-white sand stretched out endlessly, tall palms swayed in the ocean breeze, and the blue water gently kissed the empty shore.

Mary-Kate stopped, stunned. Her eyes darted everywhere. Where were Rob, Terry, and Margie? Where was the small dinghy they'd used to come ashore? Panic gripped her. *Where was everyone?*

Her eyes turned to the bay, seeking the sleek white yacht. She could see the small dinghy approach it. The people on board climbed the side, boarded the yacht. Even as she watched with disbelieving eyes, the bow turned away. It was leaving! Picking up speed, it headed for the open sea, its bow cutting through the blue water, its wake deep and wide. Leaving, and without her!

"Rob!" she yelled, furious they'd go off and leave her. How could they do that? Yet she knew even as she called his name that he couldn't hear her. The engines of the yacht were quiet, but not silent. The distance was too great.

She waved her towel, its shocking-pink color easy to see against the white sand and green background. Surely they would look back? Surely they'd remember she had accompanied them ashore? They *had* to come back for her.

The boat did not turn, did not slow. Gradually it grew smaller and smaller. Until it was gone.

"Damn! And double damn!" Mary-Kate stamped her foot on the soft, hot sand and stared at the horizon with mingled anger and disbelief. She had never expected anything like this! What was she to do now?

This was to be her grand summer. She was to be carefree and bold, returning to her normal, routine, predictable life in the autumn, with wonderful memories of tropical beaches to treasure all her life.

Except being stranded on one of those beaches had not been part of her dream.

Shaking out her towel, she folded it and looked once again to the empty bay; no help from that direction. Mary-Kate looked around the beach, taking stock of where she was. They had come to the beach from the sea, but maybe there was a road that led to town. The circle of palms seemed unbroken, though none grew so close to its neighbor that she couldn't get through.

With a last look to the empty sea, she sighed in frustration and marched toward the palms. The sooner she got in touch with the yacht, the sooner it could return for her.

She slung her towel over her arm, her only covering the white gauzy cotton cover-up she'd bought when she'd bought the bikini. The filmy material was full and gathered; first it hid then revealed her body encased in the bright pink bikini. It did not shelter her from the sun.

She'd been walking for ages on the hard-packed dirt road that had started near the deserted beach when she paused to wipe the perspiration from her face. It was hot away from the water. Fields of tall sugarcane lined the road, giving a tunnel effect as she walked along; the tall cane shut off any breeze, and funneled the heat from the sun. The hot dirt reflected the heat, and puffs of dust exploded with her every step.

Fervently hoping she was going toward something, not away from it, she started up again. She glanced at her wrist—no watch—it was on the boat.

"Along with everything else I have," she muttered. "I wish I had my watch. Damn, if I'm wishing, I'd really wish I was on the blasted boat and had never left!"

She was hot, sticky, tired. And very thirsty. Her short brown hair felt limp and bedraggled. She knew her face was probably as red as a beet from the heat. As she walked, her anger at the Lombards, and Rob in particular, grew. The summer had not been the bed of roses she had thought it would be. He and his friends had been rude, selfish, inconsiderate... She paused, wishing she'd been a teacher of English instead of maths—then she could think up dozens of adjectives to describe the obnoxious college students she'd been hired to tutor.

His parents had been no better. They were scatterbrained and impressed with their own wealth, constantly bragging about how much everything cost, and how nothing was too good for their precious son. Their idea for Mary-Kate to tutor Rob in mathematics during the cruise was a pipe dream.

Mrs. Lombard had no sense of discipline, only wanting her only child to enjoy himself. The idea of a tutor had been to appease the school, to show some sort of good faith that Rob could pass the mathematics portion required for a degree. He didn't care to work at it, and his mother drifted through life expecting everything to work itself out without the slightest bit of effort on her part.

Mr. Lombard was constantly tied up in the small communication room, tracking his vast wealth, acquiring more, and totally unconcerned with his son, wife or the guests.

As she rounded a bend, the fields opened up, and before her, on a slight rise, stood a long white house with dark green shutters flanking each window. Rambling and open, it seemed large enough to be a small hotel. Mary-Kate quickened her pace. She had to contact the yacht before it was too far away. Before it became a problem for them to return for her.

Some yards to the left of the house she saw two men working on a large truck. She hesitated, then kept on toward the house. She wanted something to drink. Then she'd have to make arrangements to rejoin the Lombards and their ship.

She still couldn't believe they'd stranded her. She wondered when they would realize she was no longer on the boat. She was sure Rob wouldn't bring the absence to his parents' attention. Once they knew she was not on board Mrs. Lombard would assume Mary-Kate would be fine and find her own way home. Maybe Mr. Lombard would miss her, only because she was someone who hadn't heard his stories six times over yet. But, depending on his mood, he could just write her off and continue the island tour.

The flagstone veranda was cool. The bougain-villaea-covered trellis overhead broke the sun's heat, the leaves gently waving as the soft sea breezes reached the house on the knoll. Mary-Kate rang the bell, and turned to survey the view. It was spectacular!

The wide blue Pacific spread to the horizon, green sugarcane fields to the left. Fields of short, squat pineapple stretched for miles to the right. The bright purple bougainvillaea framed it all like a picture postcard.

"Who the devil are you?" a voice growled behind her.

Mary-Kate turned, her eyes drawn to the expanse of tanned skin before her. The man's shirt was open, blowing back in the breeze, exposing his muscular chest, tanned deep and dark. She moved her eyes up the strong column of his neck, upward to clash with steely gray eyes. Startlingly light in the darkness of his tan, his eyes glared down at her. She glanced at his sun-streaked brown hair, then back to his chest.

His stance was uncompromising, arrogant. Fists on hips, his legs spread, he reminded Mary-Kate of a modern-day buccaneer. His shoulders were broad, muscular, his legs long and planted firmly on the terrazzo floor. He'd look more at home aboard a square-rigger than in the tropical doorway.

Mary-Kate wanted to draw her fingers down the faint dusting of hair on his chest, follow the trail as it dipped lower, until it disappeared into his tight denim cutoffs, feel the warmth of his skin, the strength of his muscles.

She took a deep breath, knowing she had a touch of sunstroke. She'd never done something like that in her life; why would she wish to do so with a perfect stranger? She'd surely be all right by morning...?

"I was stranded," she said finally, reluctantly moving her gaze back to his face. His eyes impaled her, locked on to hers, wouldn't release her.

"Are you part of that group in Hanioli Bay?" His eyes flicked contemptuously down the length of her.

"I don't know what bay you mean. We came ashore at a nice beach over there." She waved her hand in the direction she'd come from.

"I told that group this morning this was private property and to stay off. When you all came back, I threw your friends off. Where were you—hiding?"

Mary-Kate was taken aback. She'd been deserted by her own traveling companions, and this man was mad at her! "I wasn't hiding; I was around a little headland, on a smaller beach. I...I wanted a quiet afternoon. I fell asleep..." Her voice trailed off. She was trying to be reasonable, but it was hard to do with the flights of fancy her mind chose.

It was like Rob Lombard to disregard the man's warning. He had been spoiled all his life, did whatever he wished. Money could buy anything, or so he'd been led to believe. But he should have told her, at least. Mary-Kate wished she'd stayed in her cabin on the boat. Or even stayed with the rest of the beach party. At least she would be on the boat now, not facing this angry man.

How could they leave her behind?

"You're trespassing."

"Well, if I could call a cab..." Mary-Kate's voice faded as she realized she had no money. She had not expected to need any for an afternoon on a deserted beach.

"There's no cab. Just where do you plan to go?"

He surveyed her from top to toe again, lingering in appreciation at the short hemline of her cover-up.

Mary-Kate was acutely aware of how much skin showed. She resolutely stood her ground, however, refusing to give in to the desire to duck behind one of the porch chairs. He would find he could not intimidate her.

"If I could get to town, I'll arrange to rejoin the people I'm traveling with. Somehow." She was starting to question that, but refused to let her uncertainty show.

His silver eyes studied her for several long minutes, his lips a thin, tight line. Mary-Kate resisted fidgeting beneath his gaze, now knowing how some of her students felt when she gave them a certain look. She didn't like it.

She tried again. "If you could just tell me how I can get to town, I won't bother you any longer."

"There is no town. You're on a private island— my island. Your friends were told this morning not to trespass. Despite that they returned, and you with them. I find it hard to believe they'd *accidentally* leave you behind." His voice was laced with sarcasm.

"Students," she corrected absently, ignoring his tone, concentrating on her problem. "How am I to rejoin the boat, then?"

"Students?" He was thrown off stride for a moment.

"I'm tutoring one of the college students you sent away. Or I'm supposed to be. He's so tiresome, just doesn't want to do any work."

"Let me guess, the blond one," the stranger said drily.

"How did you know?"

He shrugged.

Mary-Kate waited a few seconds but, when he said nothing further, she spoke again. "If I could use your phone for ship-to-shore, maybe I could reach them that way."

"I don't have a phone you can use..."

"How am I to get back to the boat?"

"You should have thought of that before you stayed behind!"

"I didn't *stay* behind; I was left!" She raised her voice slightly as if he were hard of hearing.

"Why would they leave you?"

"They could have forgotten I went along. We don't socialize much, and this was the first time I'd gone with them on an outing."

"Or they were too drunk to remember you. They must have had a case of beer gone by the time I got there." His voice was disapproving, his stance unfriendly.

She said nothing; it was probably true. That appeared to be all the students had wanted to do—party, drink, carouse. And Rob's parents had been very lax in trying to get their son to study. One hour a day was all he spent on mathematics, and without much concentration. However, when Mary-Kate approached his parents for support for more study time, she found them displeased with her for not teaching him better—not their precious son for laziness.

"Whatever, I can't help," the stranger said.

"Who can?"

"No one here. This is a working pineapple plantation. We don't offer shuttle services to Oahu."

"But how can I get there? I can't stay here forever."

He shrugged, a gleam in his eye. "There's a supply boat that comes every few weeks. You could go on that."

He was wearing no shoes, his stance arrogant as he stood on the cool terrazzo floor. His denim cutoffs were tight, fitted snugly enough to display his masculinity, and Mary-Kate also found his expanse of muscular chest very distracting.

She was drawn to it again and again. Mary-Kate had never felt such a strong desire to touch someone, such a longing to feel the warm skin, the texture of the hair that dusted his muscular chest. Her fingers actually ached with longing. Warmth rose in her cheeks, and she forced herself to look away. She should stay out of the sun.

"When is the boat due next?" She knew even before he spoke; the sinking feeling grew worse.

"Maybe the end of the month."

"I have no clothes, no place to stay, no money. What do I do until then? That's almost three weeks away." She hoped the sudden panic that engulfed her didn't show. She would not have his opinion of her sink any lower—if it could.

He hesitated a long moment. "If that outfit was worn to attract my interest, it was wasted. I see women in bikinis all the time, though you do display yours to advantage."

Mary-Kate was stunned at his words, at the thought! The furthest thing from her mind that morning had been that she'd meet anyone, much less want to...to entice them with the clothes she wore. Before she could vent her feelings, however, he spoke again.

"I'll see if Roy's wife has some things you can borrow." He hesitated a long moment, his scowl deepening. "As to where to stay, I don't have much choice; there's room here, and to spare. I guess I'm stuck with you. But I'm not forking over any money. If you need some, you work for it; there's always work around a pineapple plantation. That is, if you really want to work.'' The last was delivered so sarcastically that Mary-Kate longed to slap his smug face.

"If I can't get back to my boat, I don't have much choice. Your wife——"

"I don't have a wife," he bit out, his eyes going hard. "And I'm not looking for one either, so your staying behind was wasted."

Mary-Kate was astonished. Did he think every woman who came his way was after him? Of all the egotistical, arrogant, conceited, self-centered individuals...

"I assure you I only want to rejoin the boat I came on. Maybe when they discover I'm not on board, they'll return for me." She spoke patiently, though her emotions were in turmoil.

"Do you plan to camp on the beach until then?" he asked dryly.

Mary-Kate shook her head. It could be morning before that party-happy group realized they hadn't seen her for a while. The thought crossed her mind that they might not return for her at all. Rob would be in no hurry to resume studies, and Mrs. Lombard would assure her husband that Mary-Kate would be fine—even accuse her of shirking her duties by jumping ship.

Then what would she do?

In the future, she'd be very wary of things that looked to be too good to be true.

"I can't stay on the beach." She sighed, anger and frustration growing. Damn Rob and his drinking, and his flighty parents! And dammit, what was she to do now? She faced the unfriendly man again, reluctant to ask anything of him.

"Can't you recommend some other place for me to stay until the supply boat arrives, or the Lombards remember to come back?"

"The houses the workers live in are small, and I don't know of any extra rooms. This place has plenty of room. Take it or leave it. I've work to do."

As an invitation, it lacked a lot. But Mary-Kate was too hot and tired to look a gift horse in the mouth. She nodded.

"Thank you." She bit the words out. There was no choice for now. She'd see what she could find out once she knew her way around. Maybe the yacht would return for her this afternoon.

"I don't know your name," she said as he stood aside with a mocking bow to let her enter. She didn't know anything about him, except that he had snarling dogs, was strong enough to expel a group of strapping college boys with no help, and was a very reluctant host.

"Dane Carmichael."

"I'm Mary-Kate O'Donnell, Mr. Carmichael; how do you do?"

"I do better without intrusions from mainland fast women who think it would be wonderful to cultivate a plantation owner. I'm not in the mood for summer romances. Call me Dane. Come on, this way, *Mary-Kate*."

"I didn't ask to be left behind," she said to his back, glaring at him as she followed. She wasn't looking for a summer romance, either. And if he owned this plantation, he was probably rich, and she had had her fill of rich men! All she wanted to do was to get home.

He was already walking down a long hall. Near the end he indicated an opened door. "Bedroom and bath." He paused at the door until she moved into the room.

Mary-Kate watched him leave; had he heard her? She was unable to figure him out. If he didn't believe her, why offer her a place to stay? If he did, why was he so angry? If he didn't want her to stay, surely some other arrangements could be made?

She turned to survey the large, airy room. It was furnished in French provincial style, a big bed in the center of the room, double dresser and side chair. A ceiling fan turned slowly in the center of the room, french doors opened to a patio. The room was simply finished, but cool and inviting. To the right she saw the adjoining bathroom with its large mirror.

She looked awful! Her curly brown hair was sticking out all over, as if she'd stuck her finger in a light socket. Her face was streaked where the salt air and perspiration had mingled. She was hot, red, with no vestige of makeup. But splashing cool water on her sticky face instantly improved things. She opened one of the drawers, and found a clean brush and comb. Dragging them through her tangled mop helped subdue it, and before long she was almost back to normal.

"Sheets." Dane stood by the bed. He dropped a set on the spread, and stood looking at her. Was his scowl permanent? she wondered. His eyes studied her; again she was acutely aware of her scanty attire.

"Dinner at seven."

"What shall I do until then?" The afternoon was half gone, but there were still hours till seven. There must be something to do. Should she stay on the beach in hope of the yacht's returning?

He shrugged. "Whatever; just stay out of my way. I'll get Roy's wife over." Without another word, he left.

He didn't plan to entertain any trespassers, Mary-Kate thought dryly when he'd gone. But she shouldn't complain; he had taken her in, albeit reluctantly. She could still be stuck on the beach.

Looked as if she was stuck here, though, until the supply ship came. Or the Lombards thought to return for her. Her anger against that group flared, and she vented her energy in activity, making the bed. The soft tropical air moved gently beneath the ceiling fan, giving an illusion of coolness to the room. It was hot, though, and she was perspiring when she finished the bed.

She wandered to the french doors and threw them open. A long, wide patio stretched out before her; tall palms at its edge cast spots of shade. Large tubs spilled colorful blooms in red, yellow and ivory. A couple of reclining chairs and white metal tables with bright umbrellas stood baking in the sun. The air was still on this side of the house, though the palm fronds rustled softly in the breeze above the house, and the sweet scents of plumeria and ginger drifted in.

Mary-Kate shut the doors, closing out the heat. Later she would open them, but not while it was so hot. She lay down on the bed, wondering what she was going to do until she rejoined the Lombard yacht. And when that might be. She ran through a variety of ways to get in touch with the errant boat, if they didn't return for her, and made plans so that she'd be prepared if they did return. Planning just what she'd tell Rob, parents or not, when she was safely on board helped her feel somewhat better.

Her thoughts turned to her host. He was angry they'd invaded his island, and, knowing how obnoxious Rob and his friends could be, Mary-Kate didn't blame him. He certainly wasn't the friendly type, though he had at least been gracious enough to put her up until she could rejoin her traveling companions.

But it seemed odd that there was no way to contact anyone. She hadn't thought anyone lived so cut off from the rest of the world.

Who was he, this Dane Carmichael? Had he always lived on this island? Why had he insisted Rob and his friends leave so suddenly? A picnic on a deserted beach seemed innocuous enough. Did he hate all visitors, or only obnoxious college kids? She didn't blame him if it was the latter. She wasn't so keen on the college kids in her party either.

Mary-Kate smiled, wishing she'd seen Dane Carmichael send Rob about his business. It was time someone put that young man in his place. And Dane had probably had no trouble. He looked strong enough and ruthless enough to do whatever he wanted. Mary-Kate remembered how he'd looked, standing in the breeze of the open doorway, his eyes light in his dark face, his shoulders broad, his light hair blowing in the breeze. Just like a pirate, a buccaneer of old: strong, ruthless, self-sufficient.

Wondering if he ever smiled, she drifted off to sleep in the hot, quiet afternoon.

CHAPTER TWO

MARY-KATE awoke some hours later, a sense of impending doom hanging over her. She glanced at her watch, remembering everything when she saw her bare arm. Of course, she was on some unnamed island, with an unfriendly, reluctant host, stranded here by Rob Lombard and his friends.

How late was it? Good grief, it would never do to be late to dinner. She'd never hear the end of it from her outspoken host. She sat up abruptly.

Someone had visited her while she slept. There were several Hawaiian dresses across the chair, their bright colors vivid against the dainty white chair. She glanced to the open door, out to the hall. She had not closed it; anyone could have walked in on her while she slept.

She wondered if Dane Carmichael had come by. What would he have thought, seeing her sprawled over the bed, scantily clothed, sound asleep? She felt vulnerable at the thought. She needed the clothes.

Closing the door, Mary-Kate held the dresses up to her. There were four, all the same style, pretty Hawaiian sundresses, loose-fitting and casual, in all colors. There was also a set of panties in a box, obviously a gift never worn. She was touched at the generosity of the unknown woman toward herself.

Twenty minutes later Mary-Kate had showered and dressed. The hours in the sun since starting her trip had brought color to her skin, light highlights to her hair. She did what she could with the limited tools at her disposal. There was no hair dryer, but a few minutes in the sun should take care of that. No makeup, but the color in her cheeks made her eyes sparkle, and she didn't need it anyway—there was no one here to impress, she told herself firmly.

Time to find her reluctant host.

Mary-Kate retraced the way to the large front room, but saw no one. Continuing through, she pushed open the screen door and stepped out onto the veranda. The trellis overhead sheltered it from the hot sun, the thick leaves of the bougainvillaea making a colorful green and purple awning. The breeze from the ocean stirred the leaves, keeping the veranda cool and pleasant despite the hot sun.

Mary-Kate sank into one of the chairs, enjoying the feel of the moist tropical air caressing her skin as it gently blew across the veranda. It was soft, warm, almost tangible. Quite different from the humid, sticky summers in Iowa. She scanned the sea. There was nothing visible—no yacht, no supply ship. Only the various shades of turquoise, jade and pale aqua of the ocean, the azure-blue of the sky, and the rich green of the island vegetation.

The silence ended as a jeep revved up the slight incline and came into view. Dane Carmichael was driving; with him in the car were two large German shepherd dogs. He pulled up before the veranda and stopped at its edge, gravel spurting from beneath his tires.

The dogs barked and jumped down, running up to Mary-Kate. She'd been around dogs all her life, so stayed perfectly still. These had to be the dogs she'd heard earlier on the beach.

"Sit, Marco, sit, Rames." Dane's authoritative voice commanded instant response. Both dogs stopped barking, and sat, their tongues panting, eyes firmly fixed on Mary-Kate.

"They're beautiful," she said as he approached. "Will they let me pat them?"

"They're guard dogs. I don't want them spoiled."

"As you like." She didn't think one pat would spoil them, but he was her host, and she wanted to keep on his good side. If he had one. So far his attitude toward her had been anything but friendly. It was barely cordial.

"Dinner will be at seven." He continued into the house. His shirt still flapped in the breeze, and Mary-Kate had trouble keeping her eyes before her, instead of following his every step.

She looked at the dogs watching her. "As if I can tell time from the sun!" she commented to the air. The dogs cocked their heads at her voice.

"He could have introduced us," she said to them, her voice soft and sweet. "I'm Mary-Kate; which of you is Marco and which Rames?"

As she said their names, their tails began to wag.

"How ferocious you are!" Mary-Kate crooned. One dog—she thought it was Marco—inched forward, soon resting his head on the arm of her chair, his eyes bright.

"Well, you are a sweetheart, aren't you?" Slowly she let him smell her hand, then reached out to pet him, scratching behind his ears, rubbing his neck. In only a minute, the other one moved forward, jostling Marco for attention. Mary-Kate laughed, and generously shared her affections with both dogs.

"Alienation of affections is against the rules." Dane's voice sounded behind her some minutes later.

She looked up guiltily. "Sorry, but they are so sweet."

"They are guard dogs; they're not supposed to be *sweet*! Here, I didn't know if you'd want something to drink, so I brought you a lemonade." He thrust a frosty glass into her hand, his fingers brushing hers, his eyes staring boldly into hers.

Mary-Kate almost dropped the glass; his touch was electrifying. She took a quick sip as he settled in a chair next to her, legs spread in a blatantly masculine way as he sprawled in the chair. He had bathed; his hair was still damp. His feet were bare, his legs long and tanned below his shorts. He wore a T-shirt, covering the tantalizing view of his chest, but now exposing the breadth of his shoulders, the smooth muscles rippling as he moved. Mary-Kate's head was spinning.

When she met his look, she quickly turned away, hoping he couldn't see her heart pounding in her chest. She had no reason to be staring. She'd seen good-looking, sexy men before—like Tom Selleck, Mel Gibson, Tom Cruise.

But not up close and in the flesh!

"So tell me about tutoring," he said, leaning back in his chair, his eyes steady.

She sighed softly and took a deep breath. "It has been a total disaster. I ought to have known it was too good to be true, but I was enticed by the vision of Hawaii, of sunny days, beautiful beaches, superb weather, sailing into the sunset on a fancy yacht."

"And the reality?"

She glanced at him, but he was gazing peaceably over the expanse before them.

"Rob needs tutoring, but would rather party. There was no support from his parents, and trying to get him to spend five minutes on mathematics was like pulling teeth. It's one thing his parents apparently cannot buy! But I've heard about everything else they can buy. Mr. Lombard is quite proud of his wealth."

"You're a maths tutor?"

Dane ran his eyes over her tanned legs, skimmed up over the short summer dress to her face. Mary-Kate was instantly and intensely aware of the skimpy dress, and her lack of under-clothing. She felt as exposed as she had in her bikini. Her blood rushed through her veins, her skin grew warmer.

"Actually, I'm a high-school maths teacher. In Ames, Iowa." She looked expectantly at him.

His lips twitched. "I have heard of Ames. Is Lombard in high school? He certainly looked older."

"College. He should be graduating now, but he can't pass the basic maths." She shrugged. "I can't tutor if he goes off and leaves me. And I don't much care. I'm pretty fed up with the way things have gone. But all my things are on their boat."

Dane took a long sip of lemonade before he spoke again, his eyes fixed so intently on her that it was almost as if he were touching her. "You don't need much here. It's always warm, and we don't dress up."

"Do you have a phone, some way I can call out?"

He slanted her a glance. "Who do you want to call? Boyfriend?"

"My parents. Maybe they can locate the Lombards and arrange for them to come back to get me. Rob probably thinks this is great—dump the teacher! Who knows what he told his parents?" She gritted her teeth in her frus-tration, her anger at the situation overcoming her awareness of the man beside her.

"He was ordered off in no uncertain terms. I don't want him back on the island." Dane's voice was hard, uncompromising.

Mary-Kate eyed the dogs. "I thought I heard dogs; I was asleep, and the yelling and barking woke me."

"You sure sleep a lot," he murmured.

So he *had* seen her asleep this afternoon. It gave her an odd feeling in the pit of her stomach. She should have closed her door. "Can I help with dinner?" She changed the subject.

"No, Nora has it almost ready."

"What do you do here, Dane?" She was proud of the easy way his name came out. Maybe he'd never know she felt as nervous as a schoolgirl around him.

"Grow pineapples."

"Sugar?"

"A few acres, but the main crop is pineapple."

"And you own all this?" she waved her hand. He finished his drink, set the glass on the veranda beside him, and nodded. "Would you show me around?"

"Why?" His voice was a shade harder.

Mary-Kate blinked. "I've never seen a pineapple plantation. I'm sure it's interesting."

"I'll get one of the men. I don't have time. You can practice flirting with him. I'll make sure he's unmarried."

"I'm not interested in *flirting*; I'm a teacher, so of course I'm interested in learning new things."

"I've had experience with teachers. I know exactly how they think and what they want to learn when they come here. And it has nothing to do with pineapples."

Mary-Kate threw him an angry look, but before she could reply he arose smoothly, lithely, and turned for the house, moving with a controlled fluid motion that reminded her of a large cat.

"You'll be called for dinner."

The screen door slammed behind him. Mary-Kate was alone with the dogs again, now wondering what he had meant about his experience with teachers. She sipped her lemonade, and speculated on her host.

Mary-Kate was called for dinner by an older woman with a huge girth and snow-white hair who introduced herself as Dane's housekeeper, Nora. The bright yellow and green muumuu covering her brushed the floor as she walked. Mary-Kate smiled to herself; if Nora ate her own cooking, she must be good at her job!

"I've a nice chicken salad and fresh hot rolls ready for dinner. Iced tea all right to drink?"

"Very much so." Mary-Kate's mouth watered as she smelled the fresh bread, and saw the nicely set table. The long oak table was polished until it shone in the spotless dining room. Fresh flowers sat in the center. Her place was set with crystal, china, silver.

Dane came in right behind her, greeting Nora politely, and waiting for Mary-Kate to sit down before he sat. His expression was more neutral than earlier, and Mary-Kate hoped dinner would be a pleasant meal.

Once Nora had served them, she left, and Mary-Kate began to eat the salad. It was delicious. The rolls were homemade and golden. Mary-Kate darted a quick glance at Dane. He was eating calmly, his eyes fixed on her.

"If the yacht returned, would they be able to contact me?" she asked.

"If someone saw them return. There are workers all over the island; that's how I knew they were here both times. They didn't return this afternoon."

She dropped her eyes and buttered one of the rolls. She was curious about Dane, but he hadn't been very forthcoming before, and she didn't want another snub.

"Where did you come from; why did you come here?" Dane asked.

"They had the yacht sailed from Los Angeles to Hawaii, and we flew to Honolulu. We've been sailing around for a month now, stopping here and there to see whatever Mrs. Lombard takes a fancy to. We spent a few days in Honolulu. I think she was trying to buy out the stores there, but she finally stopped because of lack of space on the boat."

"How long was the trip to last?"

"Another two weeks. Then I was going to take an extra few days in Honolulu before flying home. School starts in September, and I have to get ready for it."

"This will delay your plans a little. The supply ship won't be here for maybe three weeks."

She shrugged. "I'm hoping the Lombards will come back."

"I'm surprised they're not more concerned for one of their passengers."

"If you knew them, you wouldn't be. All Mr. Lombard thinks of is his money, and I don't think Mrs. Lombard thinks at all! As for Rob, he is the most self-centered creature I've met. Knowing that money can buy almost anything, it will never occur to them that I could have any problems. It wouldn't occur to them that I have no money, for that matter."

"Back to that." Dane's face hardened.

"I don't want anything more from you," she snapped, immediately knowing where his thoughts were going. "If there is work to be had, I'll do it. And I can pay you for the meals and the use of the room, too," she added defiantly.

His eyes twinkled and a slight smile tugged at his lips. "No need for all that, Miss O'Donnell. I think I can squeak through, even feeding you."

He pushed back his chair. "If you will excuse me now, I have work to catch up on." He nodded and moved to the door. Mary-Kate watched him walk away, his movements smooth and leashed, like a panther, or a leopard.

Disappointed he'd left, Mary-Kate slowly continued her dinner. She was almost finished when Nora bustled back in the room, two large strawberry shortcakes in her hands.

"Humph! Gone already, is he? He works too hard, that one. He should ease up some. The place does all right. A little relaxation wouldn't hurt. Though I guess it's more than a body can expect."

"Why is that?" Mary-Kate sat eyeing the dessert; it was one of her favorites.

"Him with a broken heart and all." Nora poured some more iced tea.

Mary-Kate sat back, fascinated. She shouldn't pry...but how intriguing. The man had not struck her as brokenhearted. In fact, the thought had crossed her mind that he didn't even have a heart.

"Oh?" Surely that was innocuous enough?

"Umm. Miss Melissa and her fancy ways. This place was not good enough for her. She always wanted Honolulu or San Francisco. They were engaged, but she broke it off."

"How sad." Mary-Kate felt a twinge at her heart. No wonder he hadn't wanted her to stay, nor was too sympathetic. He was upset over his broken engagement. She felt a little more kindly toward him.

"Maybe. Maybe she wasn't the right one for him. Who's to say? Gracious, it's been years. Time enough he should find someone else. You want anything more?"

"Nothing, this is plenty." Mary-Kate was dying to learn more, but Nora was finished. She shuffled back to the kitchen, leaving Mary-Kate to mull over the few tidbits she'd dropped. How long ago was years? What had happened to the elusive Melissa? And did that really explain why he was bad-tempered? Surely if it had been years ago, he would have got over her?

The evening loomed out endlessly before Mary-Kate when she'd finished. She carried her dishes into the kitchen, wanting to talk further with Nora.

"I was at a nice beach this morning, but it was quite a walk from the house. Is there one closer?" she asked as she put the dishes in the sink.

"Sure is, just off the back patio. Nice sandy beach, no undertows. About a five-minute walk."

"Is there a town or something on the island?" Mary-Kate asked. If she could just get to a hotel until the Lombards came for her or the supply boat arrived . . . She could call for credit on her bank card. There must be something.

"No, the compound's where we all live. It's not really a town. We have a supply boat that comes out and brings things; what you need? Dane said we were to get you whatever you needed."

"I'm fine for now. I really wanted to get in touch with the boat I came on. Dane said there were no phones."

"Too far to run the line. We've got shortwave, though," Nora said as she rinsed the last dish.

Mary-Kate wondered why Dane had not told her that. He knew she was desperate to get in touch with the Lombard yacht. Surely shortwave would work as well as a phone, maybe better? Maybe it could directly contact the ship.

"I'm off now. I'll be back for breakfast. Good night." Nora gave a cheery wave and pushed through the back screen door, the soft slap, slap of her sandals fading as she headed for home.

So the housekeeper didn't live in. Mary-Kate thought about it for a moment, wondering if she should be concerned. Shaking her head, she decided she had nothing to worry about. Dane Carmichael couldn't even stay for the full meal; he wouldn't be making any unwanted advances. Mary-Kate felt slightly piqued at the thought.

She walked slowly through the dining room, back to the living room. There were no books in sight, no magazines, no TV. The room struck her as cold—cold and austere and impersonal. It could be the lobby of a small hotel. Didn't Dane want a warm, welcoming, comfortable house?

It was none of her business. But she'd do it differently if it were up to her. She considered what changes she would make to the room to make it more appealing, more homely.

After a few minutes she gave up and walked to the front door; it was still warm and light out—maybe she'd walk to the beach. After all, she might as well make the most of the situation in which she'd found herself. A walk along a tropical beach in the moonlight would be romantic.

Too bad she was alone. It would be nice to share the evening with someone. When the image of Dane Carmichael flashed in her mind, she quickly shook her head to clear it. She would not be drawn into a fantasy starring her reluctant host, though it would be easy to do. She remembered his silvery eyes, his sexy body and the panther-like way in which he moved. Definitely *not* someone to fantasize about—too disturbing.

She found the path easily, and followed it to the beach. It was a jewel. The sand was white, fine and sparkling in the last of the sun. The water was deep blue and still. The cove was sheltered on three sides by the shore, the land encircling it as if with loving arms, opening only to the left, to the open sea. A reef beyond the opening stopped the big waves, and the water in the cove lapped gently on the shore before her.

Mary-Kate kicked off her sandals; the sand was still warm from the heat of the day. She walked along the water's edge, giving herself up to the enjoyment of the evening. The sand was a firm bed beneath her feet, as the water swirled gently around her ankles. The air was still, cooler than earlier, balmy. The palms and ferns that ringed the cove gave the illusion of primordial times. From the beach, Mary-Kate could see nothing man-made. It was as if she were alone in the world.

She sat at the far edge, where the cove opened to the sea, watching the waves crash in their mesmerizing way on the barrier reef, soaking up the peace and serenity, cares and worries forgotten. She watched until the sun set and the light faded, until only the roar of the breakers indicated the location of the reef.

The stars shone brightly in the tropical night sky, undimmed by city lights, or smog or clouds. As she walked back along the water's edge, she tried to remember the constellations she had learned as a child.

It was still early when she reached her shoes. The night was warm, the water inviting. Just beyond the palms a fat, bright moon began its nightly journey.

On impulse, Mary-Kate drew the dress over her head and waded out into the silky warm water. It was almost like a bath, the water velvety as she moved through it. The ground sloped gently, and soon she was swimming. It was heavenly. When she grew tired, she headed for shore, floating to relax, to extend her stay for as long as possible. If she were a mermaid she could dive beneath the surface and explore the enchanting depths below. She smiled at the silly dream.

"Do you need a towel?" Dane's voice startled her. Mary-Kate came instantly upright, her feet barely touching the bottom. Wildly her eyes searched for him. He was on the beach, a tall, dark figure silhouetted in the moonlight.

"You scared me," she said, conscious of her state of undress, of the awkwardness of the situation. He was standing right beside her dress! "How long have you been there?"

"A while. It's dangerous to swim alone, especially just after you eat. Shall I join you?"

"No! I mean, I was just getting out."

"Oh? I'll walk back with you, then."

Mary-Kate moved in closer. How was she to get her dress with him standing there?

"You don't have to wait for me," she told him desperately.

"I have your dress right here." Was there a trace of amusement in his voice?

"Just leave it; I'll be out in a moment."

"Why, Miss O'Donnell, I would never be so unchivalrous." There *was* amusement!

"I don't know how long I'll be. The water is so warm and nice." Please, please let him go away.

"I've all the time in the world. I needed a break from the paperwork I was doing. It's nice here. Maybe I will join you."

"No! If you must know, I have nothing on," she snapped; he was oblivious to hints.

"And I thought schoolteachers were so prim and proper! Don't you know anyone could have come by? There are over two hundred people who work on the island."

"No one did, until you came along."

"I wondered if you were wearing your suit."

"It's a great idea; I sure will from now on!"

"Joyce got you some clothes, I see? I should have asked at dinner; do they fit? She's not as busty as you."

Mary-Kate's face flushed. Great, he thought she was top-heavy!

"Roy's loss," he murmured.

She blushed in confusion. And at the awkward situation his presence caused; she was glad he couldn't see her in the darkness.

"Th-they're fine," she stammered out, willing him to leave. She could not get out of the water with him standing there! Yet she couldn't stay in all night. She was already tired, and, despite the warmth of the water, she was growing cold.

"Come on out; I'll be a gentleman this once and turn my back."

With a wary eye on the man, she moved slowly out of the sea, the water streaming, her body glistening in the bright moonlight. She felt as if she were walking out on a lighted stage.

Dane held her dress out to one side, his back directly before her. She reached for the dress. For a second he held on, then released it. Mary-Kate quickly pulled it on. It was hard to pull down over her wet skin, and once in place it molded itself to her body, the water like glue.

"Thank you," she said, "I'm decent." She wrung the water from her hair.

"Too bad." He turned to survey her in the moonlight. His face was in shadow, but Mary-Kate felt his look. He reached out and pushed back her hair, his fingers lingering on the edge of her face, on her neck. Slowly, he drew her closer. Mary-Kate was shocked at his touch, at the way her heart began pounding; she could scarcely breathe. He was so near that his body filled her senses; she could think of nothing else but Dane.

"Your skin is cool from the water," he commented ever so softly before his lips covered hers, moving persuasively.

Involuntarily Mary-Kate responded, her own lips parting slightly. But as soon as she realized what was happening, she yanked herself from his arms, staring up at him, knowing he could see her clearly in the bright moonlight, wishing she could see his face.

"And what was that for?" She was proud that her voice came out strong. None of the trembling she felt inside was evident in her tone. "Droit de seigneur?" Just because he owned the whole island didn't give him the right to make love to her.

"If you like. Isn't that why you came? I aim to keep my guests happy, give them what they want." His voice was mocking, his tone totally unrepentant.

"No, it's not why I came!"

"What game are you playing, what tactics shall we see over the next few weeks? Damsel in distress? Playing on my sympathies until your friends return for you? Hoping they don't return before I fall victim to your charms?"

Mary-Kate was stunned by his thoughts. He still didn't believe her! She stepped back another step, putting much needed distance between them.

"I'm going back." She whirled around and started up the path to the house.

He was silent as they climbed up the short hill to the house, throwing her a glance from time to time. Mary-Kate pushed herself to keep up the pace, her emotions in turmoil. How dared he kiss her? And how could she have responded? She'd just met the man that day! She kept her eyes averted from him, though her body wanted contact. She longed for the sanctuary of her room.

Dane paused at the patio edge, watching her as she mumbled a quick good night, passing him to gain her room.

She waited a moment before finding the light switch and flooding her room with light, trying to gain some control over her tingling awareness of the man. She stopped before the mirror. The dress clung to her like a second skin, molding her breasts, outlining her slim waist, her rounded hips. She eased the dress away. No wonder he had looked at her as they walked! The moonlight would not have hidden much.

She'd learned her lesson; she would not go to the beach without her bathing suit in the future, no matter how alone she might think she was. And she'd keep a wary eye out for Mr. Dane Carmichael.

She was out of the shower, wrapped in one of the voluminous towels, when a knock sounded at her door. She opened it cautiously, peering around the edge.

Dane stood before her, his eyes silvery, his tan dark in the dim light from the hall. Boldly, he pushed the door open. "I didn't think you had anything to sleep in, so I brought you a couple of T-shirts." He held out the folded cotton shirts, his eyes trailing down the toweling, resting on the soft skin at its edge.

"Thank you." She reached for them, conscious of her covering, the intimacy of the situation. While the towel actually covered her far more than her swimsuit, she felt exposed.

"About what happened at the beach..." he began.

Mary-Kate held her breath; she had deliberately not thought about that, afraid of where her thoughts would take her. She licked her lips in remembrance.

He frowned. "I was going to apologize but, if you keep looking so enticing, maybe I won't. I wonder what you look like fully clothed?"

Mary-Kate dropped her eyes, confused, heat rising in her cheeks.

"Maybe you were left behind, or maybe you stayed, hoping for more than an extended vacation. I'm willing to play the game however you want it, but understand that when that supply ship leaves you will be on it. No commitment, no recriminations, nothing beyond the days you are here."

He ignored her startled look, and drew her tightly into his arms, his kiss hard and long, his hands molding her body to his. The towel loosened and Mary-Kate clutched for it as Dane released her. Her eyes were huge as she stared up at him, her heart pounding.

"Good night, Mary-Kate." His tone was mocking. He swung away to walk down the hall.

Mary-Kate slammed the door, her knees trembling, furious at him, at herself. She leaned against the door, his words tumbling over and over in her head. He still thought she was here to make a play for him. He was toying with her, his kisses showing contempt. She had only met the man that day! He had no business kissing her at all! Though she knew rich men thought themselves above ordinary behavior. Look at Rob and his father. Dane was the same, thought he could do as he pleased, and never mind how others felt.

She pushed herself upright, glancing at the shirts he'd brought. He had the wrong impression of her, and she had done nothing to foster it. Tomorrow she'd set him straight!

Dressing for bed, she thought back on the day. She had loved the little beach she'd found when their party had come ashore that morning. The setting matched her fantasy of what a tropical beach should be: clean, soft sand, sparkling blue water, warm weather, and sweetly scented air. It was not her fault Rob had left her behind, no matter what Dane thought.

A vision of Dane danced before her—tall, brown, virile. She lightly brushed her lips, reliving his kisses, a sense of anticipation building. That way lay danger. She'd better concentrate on getting herself safely home.

Turning out the light, Mary-Kate opened the french doors to admit the warm night air. The sweet perfume of the ginger and plumeria scented the gentle breeze. Their fragrance invaded her room, evoking dreams of love and romance.

Dane's soft cotton T-shirt was large, coming well down her thighs, the much washed cotton soft against her skin, falling in folds, encompassing her. His body had touched the soothing cotton. His shoulders, broader than hers, had filled the shirt. It hung loose on her, but she hugged it to her, knowing it was rubbing her skin where it had once rubbed against his. A strangely erotic feeling bloomed with the knowledge.

She had better get away, get off the island before its magic refused to let her!

CHAPTER THREE

BRIGHT sunshine woke Mary-Kate. The sun streamed in through the opened french doors, the temperature becoming hot. The pleasant breeze of last night had gone. Mary-Kate stumbled out of bed and closed the doors, pulling the shades to block the heat. The palms were still, the sun already high in the sky.

She dressed in another of the loose-fitting sundresses, wondering if there was any kind of store around where she could purchase some things for herself. She frowned, remembering her lack of money. Dared she ask Dane Carmichael for a job? After her show of independence yesterday, what scathing remarks would he make at such a request? Yet what else could she do?

She found her way to the dining room, and was surprised to see Dane already eating, though he had papers spread out all around. Did he work all the time?

She stood in the sun from the window, its warmth pleasant. This room was cooler than her bedroom. He looked up at her, at her dress. A muscle tightened in his cheek.

"Good morning." She was better able to cope today. Her hair was clean and brushed, curly but tidy. She wasn't hot, sweaty or wet with salt water. And fully clothed. She glared at him, remembering his comment of last night. It could equally apply to him. He wore shorts again, though his cotton shirt was buttoned this morning. He still looked athletic, strong, poised as if his energy was only temporarily leashed.

"Hmm." He returned to his papers.

Was he grouchy in the morning? Mary-Kate sat at the table just as Nora entered bringing juice and fruits. When she'd been served, Mary-Kate looked over at Dane.

"Do you know exactly when the supply boat will be here?"

"Nope. Around the end of the month." He picked up another report.

"What shall I do until then?" she asked reasonably, refusing to be put off by his rudeness. She liked to plan, wanted a timetable she could work around. He had mentioned yesterday that she might work to earn some money, and, the sooner she started, the more she would have to get back to the yacht with. Maybe he'd suggest something she could do.

"No shops, no theaters, so you can't find anything to do?" He focused his gaze directly on her, his voice sarcastic, condemning.

"I didn't say that. A schoolteacher's salary doesn't provide for constant visits to stores or theaters. But I can't just sit around all day and stare at the water. You said I could earn some money. How?"

"Why did you come here?" He placed the report down, his full attention on her.

"Here? Hawaii, or this island?" She blinked, confused by the unexpected question.

"Both."

Mary-Kate took a sip of orange juice. "I took the job to see Hawaii. I thought it was the best way to get a vacation I couldn't otherwise afford. You know I was stranded *here* when you sent the others away."

"How fortunate for you," he murmured, his eyes growing cold.

"Why?"

"They had been warned away yesterday morning. They knew chances were high that they'd be sent away on their next visit. You came on that trip, then immediately hid so that when they were sent away you remained."

"Why would I do such a thing?"

"I wonder myself. I told you last night I'd play the game any way you wanted it."

"That's silly. I came for a swim from the beach, to explore around a tropical isle. I distanced myself from those adolescent studs to avoid fighting them off. Once they began drinking everyone became fair game—even old-maid schoolteachers."

"And are you? An old maid?" Dane's gaze dropped to her throat, the creamy skin of her shoulders, the soft swells of her breasts.

"Well, I'm twenty-seven and never married," she snapped.

"But looking for a husband?"

"Not some self-centered, egotistical male who thinks women plant themselves where he works to make a play for him! I never saw you before you opened the door yesterday."

"I'm not exactly unknown around here."

"Well, you are in Iowa," she retorted, angered at his thoughts.

Dane opened his lips, but the words never came.

"Now doesn't it do my heart good to see you taking a minute of time for breakfast, and with such a pretty girl, too!" Nora's cheerful voice broke in as she pushed through the swinging door and brought croissants and rolls. She was oblivious to the tension in the air, the two people glaring at each other across the polished table.

Mary-Kate dropped her eyes to her plate, avoiding Nora and Dane. Her breath came fast as she tried to get her emotions under control. He had no business thinking such a thing about her! Was he chased so much that he thought every woman was after him? Good God, *he'd* kissed *her* last night, not the other way around! And his comment that he was only trying to be accommodating, to give the tourist what she wanted, was ridiculous. What she wanted was to *leave*!

Did he really believe her skinny-dipping had been a ploy? Could he hold her accountable for his kiss?

Finally Nora pushed her way back into the kitchen, and Mary-Kate glared at Dane. "All I want is to get off this island. I want to go to Honolulu or get back on the Lombard yacht," she spat. "I never meant to be stranded here, whatever you think. Your manners are abominable, and apparently living here cut off from the rest of the world does weird things to your thought processes. I'm *not* chasing you, Dane Carmichael!"

Dane blinked in surprise at her outburst, then frowned at her.

"No one asked you here to disrupt my life."

"I'm not disrupting anything! And if you'd do something to help me get off, I'd be gone so fast you'd think I was a dream!"

He stared at her for a moment, as if lost in a trance. Finally, slowly, he shook his head. "I've got work to do."

"Nora said you had a shortwave," Mary-Kate persisted, appalled at what she'd said, knowing she had been rude. She wanted to apologize, but did not know how to do so without having him think she was only doing it to placate him.

"Nora's right, but it's on the blink right now. We're awaiting a part from the supply boat. Anything further, Miss O'Donnell? Or may I get to work?"

Without another word, Dane gathered up his papers and pushed his chair back from the table. He took another hard look at Mary-Kate. "I'd have an easier time trying to believe you if you were more subtle in your methods. Standing in the sunlight only silhouettes every delectable curve—the light cotton of the dress is too fine to do any covering.'' He watched in satisfaction as the color rose in Mary-Kate's cheeks, a gleam in his eye.

"I'll avoid the sun in the future," she mumbled, her eyes on her plate.

"Be a shame," he replied as he left the room.

"Damn you!" she whispered after him, her embarrassment fading. She glanced around to the window, knowing now why he had been staring at her earlier. Maybe she'd eat in her room in the future.

He still hadn't answered her question about what she was to do with herself all day, said nothing about a job.

Never one to mope around, Mary-Kate decided she'd wander around on her own, see what she could of the island, maybe meet some of the two hundred people who lived here, and have them explain to her how they ran the plantation, what the different jobs were, and what she might help out with until the supply boat arrived.

Though she'd rather have Dane take her.

When Nora bustled in a few minutes later, Mary-Kate smiled up at her. "Need any help?" she asked hopefully.

"No, I've been doing this for years. Why don't you go over to the compound, see the pineapples? It's a nice walk, and you'll see something of Manahakaloi."

"'Man-aha-ka-loi?'" Mary-Kate stumbled over the unfamiliar word. It was beautiful, melodious, and Hawaiian.

"This island is Manahakaloi. It's not far to the compound; turn left down the driveway, and follow the road."

Mary-Kate took the road she'd seen Dane come on the night before. She hadn't gone very many steps before one of the dogs bounded up to her, barking, tail wagging.

"Hi, want a walk?" she asked, when he sat beside her. "Which one are you? Rames? Or Marco?"

At the sound of his name, Marco cocked his head, his tail wagging.

"Okay, Marco, want to show me the island?"

Glad of the company, Mary-Kate started again. Rows and rows of pineapple stretched out on both sides of the hard-packed dirt road. There were few weeds in the neat furrows. The pineapple plants themselves were squat and bushy with thin, spiky leaves. As she walked she noticed that the center of each plant contained the fruit—soon to be harvested, if their size was an indication.

The sun beat down hot and relentlessly, and before long Mary-Kate wished she had a hat and some sunglasses. She didn't know how far it was to the compound, but she was already thirsty. She hoped Nora's idea of a short way was the same as hers!

Just when she was beginning to think she'd made a mistake, she spotted some rooftops in the distance. As she drew closer, she saw what looked like a small town. There was a big shed, dozens of small houses and a huge cinder-block building.

The flat open yard before the cinder-block building bustled with activity. Dozens of men unloaded freshly cut pineapples from the big truck pulled up by the door, and the fruit was dispatched into the building. More trucks piled high with pineapples lined up behind the first one, awaiting their turn. From the building itself came the clank of machinery, the hum of voices, and the sound of laughter.

Marco was unconcerned, so she continued, wanting to see more. Just beyond the cinder-block building, down a small incline, Mary-Kate saw the sea again. An inlet cut itself into the island, sheltered and deep. One edge extended into the water, a point for ships to be wary of. A wooden dock, tall cranes, and a row of warehouses clung to one side of the inlet.

She moved to get a better view of the small harbor, barely conscious of a clanging noise near by. Was that inlet where the supply ship would dock, load and unload supplies? There seemed to be enough equipment to do almost everything. It reminded Mary-Kate of the port in Honolulu, on a smaller scale.

"Look out!" A hard arm encircled her waist, pulling her violently against a rock-hard body. The two of them spun around just as one of the large trucks backed up, right where Mary-Kate had been standing!

Shocked, she looked up into the steely hard eyes of Dane Carmichael. Her heart sank.

"You damn fool! Are you deaf? The driver had his back-up bells on. You were right in his blind spot; he couldn't see you. That's why we have the damned bells!" Dane's voice was hard, angry.

Reaction set in as Mary-Kate became conscious of his arm around her, strong as steel, pressing her tightly against him; his chest was like granite, his long, muscular legs braced to support them. His fingers were warm and hard against her ribs. She swallowed hard, afraid to say anything as her breathing became constricted. Her body grew warm against his. She pushed against him, and was disappointed when he released her.

"I'm sorry. I—thank you for pulling me away. I was trying to see the harbor. I didn't realize what the bells were."

She hadn't been around trucks before; how would she know? With the cacophony of noise from the engines, the men yelling, laughing, and the sounds of machinery in the building, she hadn't known the clanging had even emanated from the backing truck. Nor what it meant.

"Stay with me, and stay out of trouble!" he grumbled, turning to stride beside the line of trucks. Mary-Kate paused for a moment, afraid she hadn't heard him correctly. Then she hurried to catch up. If he was going to show her around, she didn't want to miss it.

Dane spoke to each driver, verifying the loads, noting the figures on a clipboard he carried, asking about the work in the fields. Mary-Kate watched fascinated as he discussed yield and harvest rates and schedules. When he finished with the last truck, he cut across the yard and entered the large building.

Mary-Kate was hotter than ever in the yard, the heat and fumes generated from the trucks adding to the inferno. Where was the cool breeze from the ocean? She wiped her forehead.

Dane glanced down at her as she tried to match his longer stride. "You should wear a hat."

"I don't have one. Besides, you don't."

"I don't need one; I've lived here most of my life. But you'll burn if you're not careful."

His tan was dark and even. Mary-Kate's skin was pale by comparison. She would love to return home looking as dark as he did. She vowed she'd work more on her tan while she was here; there didn't seem to be much else to do.

"I'm fine," was all she said. Where would she get a hat if there were no stores around?

"Suit yourself."

"I am thirsty, though," she admitted a few seconds later.

He smiled, almost friendly, and her heart turned over. She had wondered what he'd look like if he smiled; now she knew—devastating and sexy.

"You'll love this, then. Come on over here."

She followed him into the huge building. It was the processing plant. Men and women and teenagers were standing by rows of conveyor belts, heavy machinery at one end. Endless pineapples rode shakily along the constantly moving belts. Some pineapples were picked up, wrapped in a light foam pad, and placed in cartons. Others were tossed on to a different conveyor belt. The noise level rose as they drew nearer.

Dane passed by the sorting section, leading to another area of the plant. Here huge machines stripped the prickly skin from the pineapple, coring it in the process. Dozens of women sat at high tables, slicing the fresh fruit into rings or large chunks. At another area rows of cans stood receiving the fruit. Beyond that was the juice room.

Dane led her there, and siphoned off a glassful of fresh juice and handed it to Mary-Kate, his eyes watching her closely as she drank.

It was delicious, sweet, cool and thirst quenching.

"Wonderful!" She smiled up at him, her eyes sparkling at the unexpected treat. "Much better than from cans," she murmured, holding her glass out for more.

"I've never tried it canned. I've been around pineapples all my life, first on the Big Island, then here. It's always been fresh."

"Canned juice tastes tinny." She sipped with real enjoyment. Her eyes surveyed the plant; many of the two hundred people he'd talked about must be here. Women cutting and packing, men and women testing the juices before filling the containers, others spot-checking the finished cans before they were sealed. Boxes upon boxes of packed pineapple, canned pineapple and juice containers were stacked by a loading door at the rear.

The noise level was high, the activity fast-paced and flowing.

"More?" Dane asked, his voice clearly heard above the din.

Mary-Kate smiled and nodded, holding out her glass. It was delicious. When she'd finished, he led her out of the plant to the rear, the side nearest the harbor. Two large fork-lifts shuttled pallets of boxed pineapples to the loading docks. Men on the docks covered the pallet-loads with heavy tarpaulin.

"That's where you ship from?" Mary-Kate asked, watching as men moved the finished pineapple product to the wharf. The entire operation was finely orchestrated, and larger than she had thought. And Dane owned it all. She looked at him again. Another wealthy man. She'd had her fill with Rob, his father, and those rich kids who had been on the boat. She didn't want to be around people like that any more. But she was stuck here—stuck for a couple of weeks.

"Right. We ship daily. This is the peak season, and ships are coming and going all the time to take it off while it's still fresh. During the rest of the year, production falls and the cargo ships don't come as often.''

"Could I go on one of these ships?'' Her voice brightened. The sooner she was away from this disturbing man, the better her chances of staying heart-whole and fancy-free would be. She was not looking for a summer romance. But if she had been, a voice inside suggested, Dane Carmichael would be the perfect choice.

He turned away, still walking toward the wharf. ''Afraid not. We're the last stop before the journey to Japan. A lot of our produce goes west, not east. Anyway, these ships don't take passengers.''

Mary-Kate was strangely relieved. She cast him another glance beneath her lashes; maybe she didn't want to leave. She scoffed at her thoughts, and asked how deep the water was where the ships docked.

Fifteen minutes later she was sated with facts and numbers showing the size of the operation.

"Have you owned this a long time?''

"Fifteen years. This will be the biggest year so far. I think we've reached capacity. If so, subsequent years will be about the same, if the weather cooperates.''

He walked slowly back up the incline, eyes darting from time to time to the operations around him. Mary-Kate knew he saw everything that went on, could anticipate problems and emergencies, had solutions ready.

Beyond the large yard of the processing plant started the rows of brightly colored cottages.

"Is this where everyone lives?" She was enchanted; the houses were small but in excellent condition. They were brightly painted in pretty pastel colors, and almost all of them had flowers in the front garden. It was like a tiny town.

"A few live over on the north end of the island, the rest live here."

"What does everyone do for entertainment?"

Dane's face grew hard, and he stopped abruptly.

"We manage. We have TV, books, and spend a lot of time out of doors, swimming, snorkeling, surfing. The people here talk to each other, care for each other. We don't need constant expensive, artificial activity and excitement to be content." His face was closed, his eyes steely gray.

Mary-Kate bit her tongue, wishing she'd never spoken. The friendly man of seconds ago had vanished, and only the remote, distant host she'd first met remained.

"I assure you that you'll be back in civilization before the end of the month," he went on harshly. "I think you can find your own way back? I've work to do!"

He strode off toward the plant, leaving Mary-Kate to stare after him, dozens of words trembling on her lips. She hadn't asked him to show her around; he had offered. Everything had gone well until she'd asked about entertainment, and she certainly hadn't been complaining of any lack of it.

Actually, she liked what she'd found so far. There were big differences between her life and that which she'd seen on the island. She liked the differences. She wished she could meet some of the other people here; then she'd have someone to talk to. It was hard to talk to Dane; she had to guard her every word around him. Was he deliberately trying to find fault with everything she said?

The few minutes they'd spent touring the facility had been enjoyable. She liked the way Dane had explained things to her, made sure she understood, hadn't laughed at any of her questions—and some of them must have seemed dumb. All had changed in a flash with her question. What was wrong with asking about entertainment?

She started back to the big white house. Her canine companion of earlier was not in sight. "Probably sitting in the shade somewhere," she said out loud. She passed the large doors, glancing in the processing plant to see if she could see Dane. He was nowhere to be seen. Feeling let down, she started on the dirt road back to the big house.

Her spirits rose as she walked along. It was hard to be anything but happy in such a delightful setting. She had wanted to see Hawaii all her life, and now she was really here. Seeing it, experiencing it, living it. She was suddenly glad she hadn't been with Rob and the others when Dane had run them off. She wouldn't have missed this experience for anything.

Though she wasn't sure Dane felt the same way. She wondered just what he did think. He'd kissed her, rescued her from being hit by the truck, his arm had been around her longer than had really been necessary, her softness held against his strength for endless moments. She touched the place on her ribs where his hand had rested, reliving those few seconds, her heart pounding with the memory.

She was getting obsessed with the man. Knowing wisely that it was probably due to the romance of the islands, she let herself extend the fantasy just a bit. It would end soon enough.

CHAPTER FOUR

WHEN Mary-Kate reached the house, she went straight to her room and quickly changed into her swimsuit. The sun beckoned. She'd go to the private beach and swim and sunbathe, and forget the disapproving island owner. She was on vacation; she'd make the most of it. There was a slight chance the Lombards would return for her and she'd have to leave, so she'd better take advantage of the time she had.

As Mary-Kate approached the beach, her mind recalled Dane's kiss last night. It had been a surprise, over almost before she knew what was happening. She brushed her fingertips across her lips, feeling his imprint, remembering the shock of pleasure the kiss had brought. Why had he done it?

He didn't seem to be a man of sudden impulse. He also didn't seem to like her. Not if all the subsequent encounters were anything to go by. She wasn't sure she liked him either. But she was drawn to him. He was the most exciting man she'd ever met. He constantly filled her thoughts. She frowned; she really was getting obsessed with the man.

She spread her towel on the hot sand, and dropped her flimsy cover-up. It was pleasant at the water's edge. The light breeze from the water cooled her skin, the soft slap of the waves was hypnotic. The hot sun shone from a cloudless sky. It was a heavenly day. A travel brochure could not capture a more perfect setting, she thought idly as she absorbed the scene.

Mary-Kate explored, swam, lay basking in the sun, totally relaxed. It was much better than being on the Lombard yacht. She'd learned quickly that the tutoring idea had been that of Rob's parents, not the young man in question. All he wanted to do was drink, and chase girls.

Mary-Kate had been only half a dozen years older than the others on the boat, yet next to them she'd felt ancient. Maybe it had to do with money. She had worked her way through college, and still had to budget carefully to make ends meet. While the Lombards had loads of money, they seemed to take on very little responsibility. In a truly hedonistic manner, they moved blithely through life, doing just as they pleased, concerned for no one.

She had thought she would like to marry a rich man, as all girls did, but had changed her mind once she saw how these people behaved. If all rich men were like Rob or his father, she knew she didn't want to know any more. She didn't need wealth; she wanted someone she could depend on, someone hardworking, reliable and honest.

Someone like Dane Carmichael, her traitorous mind suggested.

She pushed the thought firmly away. He didn't fit the bill. First of all, he himself had to be rich— he owned the entire island. Then he thought she wanted the bright lights of a busy city. Had that been his fiancée's reason for leaving? Nora said she'd preferred Honolulu and San Francisco. Did he condemn all women because of that?

Mary-Kate rolled over on her towel and unfastened the back of her top. She'd work on her tan, determined to forget all about her reluctant host for the time being.

When Mary-Kate awoke, the sun was low in the sky. She'd slept most of the afternoon. Without her watch, she didn't know how late it was, but it must be close to dinnertime. She scrambled up, fumbling with her top, tying the string. Her back was tight and hot. The small grains of sand clinging to her bathing suit scratched the sensitive skin.

By the time Mary-Kate reached the french doors, she knew she had a bad case of sunburn. Her back, shoulders and legs all stung as she walked. The light cover-up felt like sandpaper as it brushed against her skin when she moved. Every step became one of agony.

Quickly stripping, she took a cool shower, the water turned on low, dribbling out. It was uncomfortable on her hot skin, but it felt good to wash away the salt water and sand.

A glance in the mirror when she'd finished confirmed her worst fears; she was as red as a lobster! It would get worse, too, since the full effect usually wasn't realized until several hours later.

She pulled on panties and one of Dane's soft cotton shirts. It was almost more than she could bear. Gingerly she sat on her bed, the backs of her legs screaming in protest. Carefully she rolled over and lay on her stomach, the relief not total, but it helped.

She'd been a fool to fall asleep in the sun with no protection. She had no one to blame but herself, but it didn't help. It didn't make the pain more tolerable. Mary-Kate wondered how long it would be before the sting left.

Slowly the minutes dragged by. Her whole being focused on the throbbing sting of the sunburn. She lay still, willing her back to feel better, willing the heat to dissipate and her skin to become more supple.

"Mary-Kate?" Dane's voice called through her door. She hesitated to respond, knowing his comments about her foolishness would only add to her own self-condemnation. She debated answering, but the moment passed. He did not call again.

"Missy?" Nora knocked on the door a few minutes later, then cracked it open. Spotting Mary-Kate on the bed, she pushed into the room. "Oh, you poor child, just look at you! *Olihalui*, I have something that will help. Hold tight, missy." She shuffled out, leaving the door open.

If she did have something, it would be wonderful. Anything to stop the pain. Mary-Kate was hot, uncomfortable, and thirsty. She was always thirsty here, but now even more so. The effort to push herself off the bed and get a glass of water from the bathroom was almost too much; the soft skin behind her knees stung as she walked. Yet she did it. The water was warm, but quenched her thirst. She drank it in the bathroom, before the mirror. One side of her face was flaming red, while the other was pale. She looked a sight.

Dane strode into the room just as Mary-Kate left the bathroom.

"Oh!" she said, embarrassed to face him.

"What in hell have you done now?" he asked, his eyes narrowed as he took in her face.

"I stayed in the sun too long." She had intended to reply audaciously, but her voice cracked and the answer was almost tearful. His face softened slightly and he moved swiftly over the bare floor. His hand on her shoulder to turn her elicited a sharp wince.

"What the . . . ?" He moved behind her. "Oh, honey, I expect you're in a lot of discomfort."

Mary-Kate's heart lurched at the endearment. She met his eyes, hers wide with hurt and pain. He wasn't laughing, he wasn't condemning. His voice sounded compassionate, sympathetic.

"I am. Nora said she had something . . ."

"Aloe. The plant grows here, and will be wonderful for easing the heat and softening your skin; you'll feel better soon. I'll hurry her up." Dane gave her a gentle pat on the shoulder and left.

Mary-Kate limped to the french doors, looking out on the colorful patio, but was unable to appreciate it. Damn, she'd made a fool of herself again before the self-sufficient, competent Dane Carmichael. Any idiot knew the hot tropical sun was dangerous. Earlier he had told her she needed a hat; it would look more like she needed a keeper. Here she was, twenty-seven years old, and acting like an irresponsible little kid!

The soft slap, slap of Nora's sandals sounded as she came down the hall to Mary-Kate's room. "Here, this should help you right up." In her arms she carried a large spiky plant with fat mottled-green leaves. Placing the plant on the bedside table, she broke off one of the long, plump leaves and ran her thumbnail up to the point, exposing the gelatinous pulp.

Scooping some on her fingers, she smiled at Mary-Kate. "Turn around; this aloe will fix you right up."

The goo was cool, cold, bringing instant relief to Mary-Kate's hot, tight skin. Nora coated her legs, up her back, lifting the shirt out of the way.

"Now Mr. Dane's at dinner, you can take this shirt off, and I'll get your back and shoulders, and you'll feel much better. Don't you be worrying; he isn't going to be barging in on us."

Mary-Kate held the T-shirt to her chest, the fresh, cool aloe soaking into her skin. The relief was heavenly.

"Thank you, Nora. It feels better already." Mary-Kate was a little disappointed that Dane himself had not returned. But then, he was certainly too busy to bother with an unwanted trespasser who was too dumb to stay out of the hot sun.

"You're welcome. Dane told me to fix you up good. He knew you'd be more comfortable with me than him, with the burn over so much of your back. Let this dry, then you can put your T-shirt back on. And be able to sit down. I'll bring you your dinner."

"I'm sorry to be so much trouble," Mary-Kate said apologetically to the older woman.

"Don't be thinking that. I'm glad to help. It's a common thing here on the islands. Everyone wants to get dark as fast as they can, forgetting there's no fast way to get brown."

"Dane must think I'm a fool," Mary-Kate couldn't help saying.

"Now we don't know what Mr. Dane's thinking, do we?" Nora smiled, and went to get Mary-Kate's dinner.

Mary-Kate ate her dinner alone, upset she'd also blown her chance to have dinner with Dane. She ate alone at home, but usually had a book to read or TV to watch. Here she had a beautiful view to look out on. It was very different from Iowa. She wondered what it would be like to take all the island had to offer for granted, to know it was your home and that you would always have this beauty to enjoy—the soft breezes, endless sandy beaches and swaying palms.

Mary-Kate began to think of what she would do if she lived here. She'd fix up the house first of all, making it more friendly and warm for Dane. Maybe she could help around the office. She was a whiz at maths; surely there'd be something she could do with that? Or teach the children? She'd have to see what kind of schooling they had.

When it grew dark, Mary-Kate went to bed, carefully lying on her stomach. She fell quickly asleep, but awoke in the night, her back again stinging, hot, hurting, the discomfort waking her up. She tried to find a comfortable position, but gave it up as a lost cause.

Flicking on the light, Mary-Kate climbed out of bed and broke off a spike from the aloe plant, copying what Nora had done. She soothed the cool gel on her legs, the pain leaving immediately. If only she could reach her back!

There was a knock on her door.

She peeked out, cautiously opening the door when she saw Dane standing before her. He was clad in a pair of hastily pulled on cutoffs. His muscular chest and shoulders were directly before her eyes, strong, solid. His face was in shadow, and she blinked, trying to see him. Why had he come? She licked her lips, her gaze drawn to his body. Her fingers tingled in their desire to reach out and touch him, feel his muscles move beneath her hands, feel the warmth of his skin, the springing hair that grew down his chest toward his shorts. She drew a shaky breath, clamping down firmly on her imagination.

"Are you all right?" Dane asked when she remained silent.

"Sure." She forced her gaze up to his strong jaw, a faint stubble already showing in the lamplight, up to his silvery gray eyes gleaming in the dim light. Forcing her eyes up, she met the curious, worried look in his.

"Actually, I'm not. The sunburn woke me up."

"What did Nora do with the aloe plant?"

Mary-Kate turned and gestured to her bedside table. "It's here; I used some of it on my legs, but I can't reach my back."

"Come on, Nora's gone home long ago, so it'll have to be me." Dane walked across to her bed and broke off a pulpy spear from the plant. He watched her slowly cross the room, smiling sardonically. "Now this is a dilemma for the old-maid schoolteacher, isn't it? The moral inappropriateness of disrobing before the wild pineapple baron in the middle of the night versus chastely remaining dressed and suffering needlessly."

She smiled uncertainly, images of the two of them spilling across her mind. Before she could even say anything, however, he spoke again.

"I'll even turn around to keep your modesty intact. Though the way you're always flaunting your near-naked body around me, maybe you don't feel the need?"

"Please."

She watched as he turned his back to her, then pulled off the nightshirt and snugly tucked it beneath her arms, chest covered.

"Okay." She kept her back to him, emotions churning at his nearness.

Dane was silent for a long moment, but, just when she was about to turn around to see what he was doing, Mary-Kate felt the cool, soothing gel from the plant on her hot shoulders. His fingers were gentle and smooth as he spread the remedy over her shoulders, over her back. His hand was warm; she could feel his touch through the gelatinous substance. Smoothing over her back, tracing her spine, slipping along the sides where the skin was not burned, his fingers were warm against her heated skin. Tantalizing in their touch, the feel of them skimming across her body caused her breathing to suffer. She forgot about her sunburn, her legs began trembling. Could she maintain a calm demeanor, concentrate on not making a fool of herself over a man's touch— this man's touch?

Mary-Kate felt ripples of delight through her entire body, though his fingers barely skimmed her back. His touch brought her unknown longings, a strong desire to turn around and draw him to her. To feel his lips against hers again, to feel his lips on her body, kissing away the hurt of the sunburn, kissing her to the heights of rapture and passion.

She moved; this had to stop—it was too dangerous.

"Umm, thank you," she murmured, stepping away, at once both yearning for him to continue until morning, and knowing he'd have to stop and leave before she did something silly.

"Feeling better?" he said softly, his fingers resting on the small of her back, just above her panty-line. His hand was hot, his touch burning in a way the sunburn never could.

No, she wasn't feeling *better*; she was feeling hot and breathless and desirable and shy. But she couldn't tell him that!

"Thank you, my back is much better——" Her voice broke and she took another step, breaking contact. She bit her lip; would he leave now? She needed to get dressed, pull her shirt on, regain some semblance of normality; but not with him watching. The silence dragged on and Mary-Kate chided herself for acting so gauchely. Heavens, he'd surely seen a woman before; would the sight of her drive him wild with passion and lust?

"Are you thirsty?" he asked.

"Yes, I can't seem to get enough to drink."

"The few times I've been sunburned, I've been very thirsty. I'll get you something."

She heard him move away, move down the hall, and she quickly donned the T-shirt, her relief almost tangible. For a reckless moment she wished she had a glamorous diaphanous nightgown that would drive men wild, instead of his huge T-shirt. But it would do nothing but give him further fuel for his mistaken impression that she was after him.

She drew up the sheets and moved away from the bed. The proximity of the man and her bed were too tempting. She needed some room. Mary-Kate opened the french doors, and stepped out onto the patio. The air was cool, fragrant. The leaves and petals of the bright flowers cascading from their containers stirred slightly in the nighttime breeze. The bright moon contended with the light spilling from her doorway to illuminate the patio, giving everything a silver sheen. The palms were tall, silhouetted sentinels guarding the island paradise. Mary-Kate took a deep breath, enraptured with the setting.

Dane found her there, feasting her eyes on the scene, trying to imprint each moonlit detail to memory. She would not always have this sight to enjoy. She wanted to treasure every memory for the long, cold winters in Iowa.

"Here you go—iced tea, and hot chocolate."

"Iced tea sounds great, but why hot chocolate?" She reached for the glass and greedily drank down the icy beverage. Who would have thought she'd spend a romantic evening beneath the moonlight in Hawaii with a good-looking, sexy man while wearing an oversize T-shirt?

He stepped closer, his nearness overwhelming. Mary-Kate needed to breathe as tension rose within her. "Help you go back to sleep," he explained.

"How did you know I was awake?"

"My room's right there, next to yours. I saw the light come on, and figured out why."

"I was stupid to fall asleep at the beach," she confessed, sipping the last of the tea.

"It happens. Next time take an umbrella, and at least sleep in the shade. There's one in the hall closet." His voice was lazy, soft, intimate. There was no trace of the scathing condemnation she expected to hear from him, nor the hateful, mocking tone he sometimes used. Idly she wondered if he saved that for when she was in fighting form. If so, it showed a sensitivity she had not expected. She looked up at him in the moonlight; had she misjudged him?

"Here, now drink your chocolate."

He took the glass from her hand, his fingers brushing over hers, slowly drawing the glass away. Mary-Kate felt butterflies kick in her stomach. She darted another glance up at him, and quickly looked away when she saw his look.

The hot chocolate was creamy, thick and rich. It was made with dark chocolate, and tasted almost like a melted candy bar. She sipped it slowly, feeling its warmth permeate her body, warming her again, relaxing her. It would not be hard to fall asleep, unless thoughts of her host kept her awake.

"This is a lovely time of day—er—night," Mary-Kate said, tracing the rim of the cup with one finger. "It's cool, and the air is so soft and scented. I love it."

"It's a good time to walk along the beach; want to go?"

It was tempting; Mary-Kate looked at the pathway, evoking visions of the two of them along the beach. Would he kiss her again? At the thought, her heart slammed against her ribs, beating in double time. She had to stop that foolishness immediately. She was only here until the Lombards returned for her, or the supply ship came. She could not give in to the temptation to spend more time with Dane Carmichael. He had already shown her what he thought about her. Rich men didn't fall for schoolteachers, and their life-styles were not something she admired anyway. Better she put distance between them. She wanted to be more herself before facing such temptation, so that she could be sure then that she could resist.

"Maybe another time?"

"Scared?" he guessed.

Was she so transparent? "When I'm feeling better," she bluffed.

Dane stepped back into her room, and broke a small leaf from the aloe plant. "I didn't do your face."

"I could do it myself," she murmured, making no effort to take the leaf from him, no effort to release the cocoa cup.

"Part of the service." His voice was low, and sweet as honey. Gently he traced her cheek, smoothing the aloe over her skin, from her forehead to her jaw, lingering to rub her jaw gently with one thumb long after the aloe was spread.

His face dropped lower, blotting out the moon, blotting out the shimmery sky. His lips touched hers, and Mary-Kate forgot everything. The warmth of his lips touched her heart and she remained still, letting the sweetness of the moment invade her, embrace her, excite her.

The rich scent of the tropical flowers etched their mark on her memory. The feel of the balmy night air against her skin enhanced the ethereal magic Mary-Kate experienced. It was a dream time.

Dane's lips were warm, firm, drawing a response from her that surprised Mary-Kate. Her body grew warm, her awareness of everything else dimmed, and only Dane remained.

He pulled back slowly, then traced her lips lightly with his thumb, staring down at her, his face in darkness. She wondered what he was thinking.

"Now, just why are you here, I wonder?" he said softly at long last.

"I was left behind." Didn't he believe her yet?

"As a present for me?" His voice was whimsical.

"Thank you for helping me. I couldn't have put the aloe on myself." She tried to ignore the lovemaking, tried to sound normal, unconcerned.

"Good night, Mary-Kate."

She drifted to her room, slowly closing the french doors and the hallway door, still caught up in the magic he wrought. It wasn't fair. To him it was only a game. In seconds Mary-Kate turned off the light and climbed into bed. It was hours, however, before she slept.

CHAPTER FIVE

ONCE the aloe had been applied the next morning, with Nora's help, Mary-Kate was able to don one of the cotton dresses loaned to her. The day loomed endlessly before her, and she didn't know what to do, since she was reluctant to go out of doors. It would be several days before she'd want to risk the sun again. And she'd be a lot more prudent in the future.

Mary-Kate slipped quietly into the dining room. Dane was already eating, but glanced up when she appeared, watching her from enigmatic eyes. Mary-Kate swallowed hard and, avoiding the sunlight streaming in, moved to sit at the second place. She ignored Dane's look.

"Sleep all right?" he asked. She nodded, keeping her eyes firmly on the coffee she was pouring. "How's the sunburn this morning?"

"Still sore, but better. At least I can sit down now." She reached for some of the fruit. Dane had the bowl ahead of her, and handed it to her, his fingers deliberately brushing against hers.

Mary-Kate's heart lurched and she peeked up to find his gaze locking with hers. For endless, breathless moments she felt suspended in time. She pulled her eyes away and blinked at the fruit.

As if in slow motion, she scooped some mango, papaya and passion fruit onto her dish.

She had never been so conscious of another person in her life. Her very being was attuned to his every move. She could hear his soft breathing, see his chest rise and fall, imagine that the warmth she felt emanated directly from his body.

Darting him a quick look, she saw the gleam in his eyes, as if he knew exactly what effect he was having on her.

Affecting a nonchalance she didn't feel, Mary-Kate ate. But the food had little taste, and she had to force herself to chew, to swallow, to drink. Casually letting her eyes move around, she twice looked at Dane, finding his eyes steadily watching her. It was unnerving!

Mary-Kate put down her spoon. She couldn't continue. Her nerves were stretched too tightly.

"Finish your breakfast, then join me in my study," Dane said, rising.

She nodded, afraid to trust her voice. She felt as if she'd run a mile. Sagging back against the chair, she relaxed for a moment. She had better get a grip on herself before she made a total fool of herself before Dane Carmichael.

Deliberately taking her time over breakfast, she lingered over a second cup of coffee. She wondered where the Lombards were, and why they had not returned for her. Had they just gone blithely on their cruise, assuming she'd be fine? Deciding she'd delayed long enough so that Dane would not suspect how much she wanted to see him, she left the table and sought the den.

It was easy to find—along the hall opposite to her bedroom. On the wall opposite the door was a bank of windows overlooking the front of the house, first the small green lawn, then, beyond, the blue Pacific. To the left was Dane's desk, his file drawers, a computer, and rows and rows of books. To the right, more books and a couple of easy chairs. Recessed in the corner was a large color TV.

"I've finished," she said, stepping into the room.

He rose and came around the desk, his approach making Mary-Kate feel weak at the knees. She sidestepped toward the right, pretending to be looking at the books, conscious of his movements, the long length of his legs, the powerful muscles in his arms and shoulders, the dark tan of his skin, the lovely silver of his eyes. She swallowed, and threw a nervous smile over her shoulder.

"This is great—the beautiful view, all your books. It reminds me of a library. How nice to be able to look out over the ocean like this." She was disgusted with herself. She was acting like a nervous schoolgirl caught in wrongdoing.

Dane smiled devilishly, his eyes dancing at her discomfort. "You're babbling, Mary-Kate; are you nervous?"

"No; should I be?"

He was close now; Mary-Kate had to tilt her head back to see him. He was too close; she wanted to step back, but held her spot. She would not give him the satisfaction.

She opened her mouth ready to let him know she did have some sense, but paused before snapping out the words. He was right; she'd been a fool to overreact the way she had. She didn't need to compound that now by hasty words.

"Yes, I think you're right," she said meekly, to his great delight.

"I'm surprised to find you in agreement with anything I say."

"I'm not usually, am I? But when you're right, you're right. Where did you get all these books?" She looked up at him, her eyes soft as he replied.

"Some I brought back with me when I visited the other islands, some I've ordered." He broke off, staring down at her, his eyes growing steely.

"Stop that!" he ordered abruptly.

Her eyes widened. She took a ragged breath. "Stop what? I was listening to you. You were talking about where you got the books."

"If you don't stop looking at me that way, I'll think you want me to kiss you again," he said dangerously.

Mary-Kate looked away, shocked at how much she wished he would. She felt drawn to him as if silken bands were surrounding them, tightening, pulling them together. It had to be the magic of the islands. She turned back, gazing at his mouth as he spoke, remembering the touch of his lips on hers. His voice was smooth and deep. She could lose herself in what he was saying.

"Mary-Kate, I'm warning you."

She turned away and moved to review the books on the shelves. She was already cast as throwing out lures to him; she would not add to his picture of her. Reading the titles, she was struck by the mix she found. There were numerous books on agriculture, on pineapples, sugar, plant diseases and tropical flowers, which she might have expected. Then there were spy thrillers, mysteries, and an entire shelf devoted to romances.

"I didn't picture you liking love stories," she murmured, drawing one from the shelf.

"Those are Nora's; she likes to read them. I pick up a few new ones from time to time for her, and she likes to reread some of her old favorites. If she's waiting for laundry to be finished, or just taking a break, she'll read some." He was working at his desk, and was only paying scant attention.

Mary-Kate continued her study of the room, spotting a large picture on one table—a woman, a man and two boys. The younger boy looked a lot like Dane.

"Your family?" she asked.

"Yes."

"I didn't think you'd have one," she commented.

He looked up at that, a scowl on his face. "What did you think, that I hatched from under a rock?"

She smiled and cocked her head, as if considering. "I guess not, but you seem so self-contained somehow that I just didn't picture you with parents. Where do they live?"

"My father lives on the Big Island. My mother is living in Europe with her current husband. That picture is old. She left years ago. She's been married six or seven times since then. Always looking for more. More money to have more fun. Never content to stay and build something, she has to have constant entertainment, and excitement at every door." He glared at Mary-Kate for a moment, then looked back to his work. "Do you have parents?"

"Sure. One of each; they are still married, live in Des Moines. I see them at Christmas. Other summers I've spent some of my vacation with them. I have two sisters, too. I'm the youngest."

"I'm the second son. No sisters."

He turned back to his calculations, dismissing Mary-Kate. But she felt she'd learned something important. His mother didn't live on the islands. Nor had Melissa wanted to. Did he think all women felt that way? Was that why he thought she was looking for entertainment?

She watched his bent head for a minute, wishing she could say something that would interest him, that would make him want to talk to her, to find her fascinating, more fascinating than his spreadsheet. She sighed and turned to sit gingerly on one of the chairs, opening the book.

From time to time Mary-Kate glanced up to find Dane's eyes on her as she sat reading in the large, comfortable chair. She'd smile and return to her book, each time finding it harder and harder to pick up the story line. She was very aware of him physically as he sat at the desk. He looked too wild and free to be content behind it. He should be out striding about the land, giving orders to his men, fighting the elements.

Some time later Mary-Kate felt his eyes on her again. This time she looked up from the book to meet his gaze. Raising her eyebrows in silent question, she stared back at him.

"You've been silent for more than two hours," he commented, his expression guarded.

"You've been working," she replied with a shrug.

He tilted back in his chair, playing with a pen. "Unusual."

She shook her head. "Not really. I had something to do, and you were working. Remember, I'm not supposed to disrupt your life," she teased.

He cocked an eyebrow at that, a trace of a smile touching his lips.

"There's disturbing and there's disturbing. Talk is not the only distraction." He abruptly sat up, scowling. "I'm going down to the wharf. Stay here if you want." He picked up a folder and walked out of the study without another word. Almost as if he was angry.

Mary-Kate stared after him. Why would he be angry? she wondered. She had been engrossed in her book, not bothering him. Could he not even bear to have her in the same room?

Yet what about the kiss last night? She let the book fall forgotten to her lap as she relived that kiss, the kiss they'd shared. Thinking about it caused her heart to race, her lips to tingle and a slow bud of desire to grow. Mary-Kate smiled in remembrance. She'd like to have another one. But he only reacted in the moonlight. Could she get him out into the moonlight again? Would he ever be friendly by the light of day? She sighed and returned to her book, wishing real life were as predictable as it was.

In the afternoon, it rained. One minute it was sunny and warm, the next a dark cloud blew across the sky and a torrential downpour soaked the patio, the ground, drummed on the roof. Nora hurried around to shut the windows, and it soon grew hot and stuffy in the house. Mary-Kate went to stand in the front door. The overhang sheltered it from the rain dancing on the veranda, and she stood for a long time watching it saturate the ground, bend the palm fronds and flatten the flowers beneath the weight of the fat drops. The humidity rose and she felt the closeness in the air.

The storm didn't last long, passing away as swiftly as it had come. It was cooler when the rain passed. The sky became blue again as the dark storm cloud continued out over the water. Steam rose from the ground in the hot sun.

Dane did not come to dinner that night, but remained at the compound. Mary-Kate ate at the dining-room table, but she had a book on the history of Hawaii, and hardly missed the man. She would be happy for the rest of her stay with the library he owned. The assortment was varied and most of the books of recent vintage. After she finished the history, she wanted to read the book on the plant life of the islands and tropical fish.

Nora left shortly after dinner, and Mary-Kate was alone in the big house. She turned on the lights in the living room, and read for a while. When she grew sleepy, she decided to go to bed.

The door to Dane's room, just beyond hers, was open. She hadn't known which room was his until he'd told her on the patio last night. Curious, she wondered what his room was like. Stopping at her door, she paused in indecision. It surely couldn't hurt to take just a peek. With a guilty glance over her shoulder, she walked further down the hall, stopping at his open door.

Dane's room was similar to hers in size, but his bed was bigger, his furniture of sturdy oak. The terrazzo floor was bare, no rugs to soften its austerity. He also had french doors leading to the patio. She stepped inside. On his bedside table was a book—a mystery, she saw when she drew near enough to read the title. He kept his room neat, or perhaps it was Nora. It was spotless. The french doors leading to the patio were open, the warm night air inviting.

It must be nice to live where you never had to worry about locking things up, Mary-Kate mused as she wandered around.

"Care to stay the night?" Dane asked.

She whirled around, her heart sinking. He was standing squarely in the doorway, nailing her with his steely glare. His gaze was hard, insolent as he let his eyes drift down the length of her. Again she was reminded of a pirate.

"I just wanted to see more of the house," she said, licking her dry lips, hot with embarrassment. She wished she could sink through the floor. No wonder he'd spoken as he did, finding her in his room. It was a likely interpretation of her presence.

"You could have asked Nora for a tour; I'm sure she would have shown you around." He stepped into the room, and closed the door behind him with a loud click. His eyes never left hers.

Mary-Kate stood her ground, though her impulse was to flee through the open french doors. She could run to her room and close her doors. And what would stop him from coming through if he wanted to? a small voice asked.

"The door was open..."

"It usually is. When I don't have guests, I don't close it." He took another step.

Mary-Kate clasped her book before her, watching him, mesmerized, as he took another step, his face closed, inscrutable, his eyes a dark glint. What was he thinking? Did he really think she wanted to stay the night with him? Or was he deliberately trying to embarrass her?

For a moment a picture of the two of them together in his bed flashed through her mind, and she darted a quick glance at the bed and back to him.

His eyes had a light in them she'd not seen before. Before she could think, she stepped back, toward the french doors. She swallowed hard. "I'm sorry, Dane. I shouldn't have come in. I just wanted to see more of your house. I . . . good night."

Before she could escape, his hand snaked out and grabbed her arm in a hard grasp, drawing her up to him, his eyes narrowed.

"Be a shame to leave now, Mary-Kate. What else did you want to see in my room?"

"Just how it was furnished. It's very nice," she told him lamely. He stared down into her eyes; she couldn't look away.

"I don't know who you are, Mary-Kate, or what you're up to. You tantalize me, then retreat. Are you a tease, or genuine?"

"I'd better go," she said, pulling ineffectively against his hand.

Her eyes moved, locked with his. She couldn't look away, couldn't draw back. His fingers gentled against the sensitive skin of her arm. His eyes gazed down into hers, and slowly his head lowered. Involuntarily Mary-Kate rose to meet him. His lips were cool, firm, familiar. With a soft sigh, Mary-Kate gave herself up to the enjoyment of his embrace.

His hand moved to her back, but the slight sting of sunburn was lost in the excitement of his touch. Mary-Kate moved closer, savoring the feel of his hard chest pressing against her, his strong legs braced to hold them both. Her hands crept up to the column of his neck, threading through his thick, sun-streaked hair. Her fingers had a will of their own as finally they could touch as they had longed to. His skin was warm, smooth, tight over supple muscles, his hair thick and springy.

Dane released her mouth and placed hot kisses along her neck, tilting her head for the vulnerable pulse in her throat.

"Are you staying?" he asked softly.

With a start, Mary-Kate pulled back. Her breasts were swollen with desire, there was a longing deep within her she'd never felt before. It would be so easy to stay, so glorious.

But she couldn't.

"No...I can't..." She stepped back, and his arms released her without protest. Turning, Mary-Kate fled. Gaining her own room, she stood in the dark for long moments, fingers across her lips, wondering if he'd come after her. Yearning for him to do so, afraid he would. She was strongly attracted to him. Who wouldn't be? He was sexy, virile, and handsome as the devil, a man of power and direction. Incredibly good-looking with his dark hair, tanned skin and light eyes, he drew her like a magnet.

Strong attraction wasn't necessarily lasting. And he didn't care for her. Sexual attraction, no matter how strong, wasn't enough for Mary-Kate. She wanted love, and love had to be a two-way street.

But one night with Dane Carmichael would probably be glorious!

When Mary-Kate awoke the next morning, she felt better. Her back was still sensitive, but the pain and discomfort had gone. After her shower she looked at it in the mirror. Her skin was still more pink than brown, but was gradually changing. Maybe she wouldn't peel.

The dress she wore today was bright blue and pink. It was slightly more snug than the others she had worn, and fitted her as if it had been made with her in mind. Her hair curled around her face, her eyes sparkled, but she refused to think about why they did. One cheek was darker than the other, but she'd make an effort to keep the pale side in the sun over the next few days and even it out.

Dane had finished breakfast and gone when Mary-Kate entered the dining room. Her face lit with a big grin, however, when she saw the hat and suntan lotion at her place. There was a note.

Wear the hat if you go out. The lotion should protect you.

She tried the hat on. It was pink and white and had a wide, floppy brim. Setting it on her head, she looked for a mirror. It was cute. Where had he come up with it?

She ate breakfast, and went to the study to get another book, one on skin diving. Mary-Kate had read several during the spring, once she had signed up as a tutor. She had so wanted to do some diving in Hawaii. The water was clear and warm with hundreds of varieties of fish and plants, ideal for skin diving. Maybe she'd still get a chance.

It was pleasant to sit on the shaded veranda, to feel the cool ocean breeze and read her book, or stare off into the distance. The breeze seemed stronger than usual, but it kept her cool. The morning passed swiftly. Before she knew it Nora brought her a fruit salad and some warm rolls for lunch.

The afternoon stretched out before her, and Mary-Kate was debating whether she dared try the beach again, this time lathered up and protected, when she heard the jeep.

She watched as Dane barreled around the last curve and came to an abrupt stop before the veranda, gravel spurting. Did he ever drive slowly and ease to a stop? She didn't think it was his style. He climbed down and walked over to Mary-Kate.

She watched him approach, suddenly aware of happiness bubbling up within her at the sight of him. Watch it, girl, it would not do to fall in love with him. He'd made his feelings very plain.

"The surf's up, and some of us are going surfing; want to come?" he asked, pulling a chair up beside her and sitting on its edge.

"I don't surf."

"If you want to learn you can try it, if not, you can watch."

"Are you going now, in the middle of the afternoon?"

"Sure; the tide is right and the wind's stronger than it's been lately. Should make for good waves, for this time of year. Winter's the best time for the big waves. Get on your swimsuit; I'll be ready to leave in a few minutes."

Mary-Kate hurried to change, smiling at Dane's enthusiasm. Gone was the disapproving man she'd last seen. He seemed like a kid playing hookey for the day.

She pulled on her swimsuit, a trifle nervous wearing it before Dane. There was not much to it. She put on her cover-up, wishing it was longer, thicker. A nice floor-length terry-cloth robe would be just the thing, she thought. But this was Manahakaloi, not Ames, Iowa, and she was on vacation. She grabbed her hat, the lotion, a towel, and left.

Dane was already on the veranda, wearing his cutoffs and a shirt. He turned when he heard Mary-Kate, his eyes appraising as she walked toward him. His eyes traveled down the length of her, lingering on the dark shadow between her breasts, the long, silky legs.

Dane frowned and took the lotion from her, gently pushing one shoulder to turn her around. "Take off your cover-up, and I'll put lotion on your back. You don't want to get burned again." His voice was gruff.

Mary-Kate complied, shy and self-conscious. Her suit was very skimpy. The bra was only small wisps of bright hot-pink material covering her full breasts. He'd called her busty; did he think her breasts were too large? The pants were low cut, revealing almost more than they concealed. When swimming, she sometimes wondered if they would come off.

The touch of his fingers smoothing on the suntan lotion was soft and sexy. Her skin responded to his touch, nerve endings quivering, clamoring for more. He could smooth lotion all over her body, kiss her again . . .

Mary-Kate willed herself to stand still, not to give in to the weakness that invaded her knees, to ignore the sudden increase in her heart rate. Breathe in, breathe out.

Her senses focused on the feel of Dane's fingers as they traced patterns of delight across her back, along her waist, to the top of her briefs like small flames competing with the fiery heat of the sun. Maybe she should go in and lie down, until this feeling of lassitude and desire passed.

Dane's hands smoothed, soothed, kindled a flame over every inch he touched. Tracing her spine, his touch changed; it no longer soothed, but instead ignited sparks. When his hand continued down, she moved slightly, unable to continue placidly. Had he any idea the torment he was causing?

"Here." He thrust the bottle into her hand, and moved away, his face averted. "Finish up, and let's go."

Mary-Kate spread the lotion on her legs and stomach. Conscious of his eyes watching her, she took her time, drawing out the movements, showing off just a little as she propped her foot on the chair, smoothed the lotion slowly over her tanned legs—taking perverse pleasure in behaving as sexily as she knew how. She wondered if he had been immune to the sensations his touch had caused. It didn't help her heart rate, or her concentration, to know he'd done it deliberately. Would this have any effect on him?

"For God's sake, finish up and let's go!" Dane's voice was ragged.

Putting on the cover-up as soon as she was finished, she gathered her things and, without looking at Dane, climbed into the jeep, satisfaction deep and complete.

CHAPTER SIX

"THANKS for the suntan lotion and the hat," Mary-Kate said as Dane climbed into the jeep.

"No problem. Hope it helps." He gave a piercing whistle, and the two dogs bounded around the corner of the house and scrambled into the vehicle. With a quick glance at Mary-Kate to make sure her seat belt was fastened, he backed the jeep around and started off down the slight hill at an alarming rate.

From terrific to terror in three seconds, she thought, holding on. The scenery whizzed by at great speed. There were no doors or top to the jeep, and she felt catapulted through air. She pulled her seat belt tighter.

"Where do you surf?" she yelled over the rush of the wind.

"Toward the northern part of the island. The waves are bigger there, and the beach smooth and debris free."

"Do you surf alone?"

"No. It's not safe. A person can wipe out and get hit by his board. There needs to be at least one other person. As it turns out, several of the employees here this summer love to surf. We work pretty much the week around during the peak season, and catch time here and there as we can, when the surf's just right.''

''But winter's better?''

''Yes, winter's better. The workload is lighter. We can go surfing for days on end, if we want. Care to try it?''

''I'll just watch, at first.'' Mary-Kate wasn't sure she wanted to be at the mercy of crashing waves. She liked the idea of swimming under them with scuba gear, but not balancing on a floating board and riding them in. Still, she enjoyed watching people surf, and was intrigued to see someone she knew doing it. She knew Dane would do it very well.

The road split and Dane took the turn to the right. Soon the open fields of pineapple gave way to the high growth of sugarcane. Again, Mary-Kate felt as if they were in a tunnel, with the roof open to the sky. There was no view, only the road ahead, the sky above, and tall walls of green. Before long, however, they turned on another dirt road, and ahead of them lay a large, wide, white sandy beach.

A dozen or so men and women were on the shore, some wading in the shallows; others were already on their boards, catching waves. Several people waved as Dane drew the jeep up beside others, and he waved back.

''Where's your surfboard?'' Mary-Kate asked, as she stepped down. There must be thirty people or more.

"Over there; Mike brought it for me. I keep it at the plant, since I'm usually there when we decide to take off." He paused a moment, looking at her through narrowed eyes. "Come on; I guess I have to introduce you."

"Don't put yourself out," she muttered, throwing him an angry look.

"People immediately begin to think things—things that aren't true," he said bitterly.

"Shall I just mention I don't even like you?" she snapped. It wasn't her fault if people thought things. Why take it out on her?

"That'd be just fine." His look was equally angry. "Damn, I shouldn't have brought you!"

"Oh, for heaven's sake, so they talk a day or two. Once I'm gone, they'll know their precious boss was in no danger from the Iowa schoolteacher."

He grinned suddenly, his eyes going silvery. "I don't know about that."

Mary-Kate was suddenly confused. She looked away, at the people staring at them.

As Dane made the introductions, the names started to swim in Mary-Kate's head. There were over two dozen people on the beach and another half dozen still in the water. She smiled and greeted everyone, remembering only a couple of the names.

She wondered what they did think about her, knowing that, even if Dane had said nothing, Nora would have told her friends about the unwanted visitor, about all the trouble she was causing. What would be the talk at the compound tonight?

There were no sly looks, no knowing glances, and Mary-Kate relaxed. Maybe Dane was seeing things that weren't there. She enjoyed the afternoon.

When Dane took off for the water, she spread her towel near an obviously pregnant woman named Lisa.

"I love to surf," Lisa said, smiling a welcome at Mary-Kate, "but can't right now. I should be back in shape when the good waves come in the winter. That's my husband out there to the right—Mike."

"He and Dane are friends?" He was the one who had brought Dane's board.

"Yep. Been friends for years. Dane's a bit of a loner, especially since Melissa left. Mike is about as close as Dane will let anyone get. We live here the whole year round. Though once the baby is older I guess we'll have to move to one of the bigger islands."

Mary-Kate heard the name of Dane's fiancée again, and longed to inquire after her. Would Lisa volunteer anything?

"Melissa?"

Lisa flashed her a look, then nodded slowly. "Sorry, you wouldn't have known. Melissa and Dane were engaged once, about four years ago. She broke it off after staying here for a few days. She didn't like Manahakaloi—too boring for her.

She wanted to help Dane spend his money elsewhere.''

Mary-Kate kept her eyes on the surfers, afraid to say anything that would stop Lisa recounting things past.

"Dane loves it here; it's his baby. He started the plantation as a kid, and has really brought the place along. There's no way he'd be a token owner, just stopping by occasionally. He did everything for her—built that house, let her furnish it. But it wasn't enough."

"Melissa didn't want that?" Mary-Kate looked at Lisa. Was she staying in Melissa's room? Did the coldness of the house reflect Melissa? Maybe Dane was better off without her.

"Nope, she wanted to live in San Francisco, travel around the world, buy expensive things. She met Dane through his mother, and wasn't at all content to stay on a slow-moving island. It's the bright lights and excitement for Melissa Hargraves."

"But it's so nice here."

"I know; I love it."

"Why would you want to move to one of the bigger islands? This one seems perfect."

"No schooling here. Some of the parents do their own tutoring, especially when the kids are young, but once they get older it's time to move to a bigger place that has a good school system."

"Aren't there enough children to hire a schoolteacher?"

"Dane's tried it three times, and it's never worked. The teachers he hired either found it too isolated here, or there were not enough materials, or nowhere to go for field trips, or not enough salary, or not enough to do. Just a lot of excuses, if you ask me. I think they thought to live in paradise and make a play for our gorgeous boss. When they found him unavailable, they cut their losses and ran for the Big Island."

Mary-Kate searched the surfers in the sea until she found Dane, out beyond the edge of the breakers, sitting astride his board, waiting for a wave. No wonder he was wary of her motives. To him she was another schoolteacher whom he thought was making a play for him.

She tilted her head stubbornly. She'd given him no reason to suspect she was trying to make a play for him, despite his thinking she had deliberately remained behind when Rob and the others were told to leave. She would show him she was one schoolteacher who was immune to his charms!

"How many kids are on the island?" Mary-Kate asked.

"We have twenty right now; fourteen are of school-age. I think if there were good schooling here some of the older workers that left would return. Everyone likes it here. There's no crime, everyone's friendly. The work is a little monotonous, but the way of life makes up for it. Dane rotates people, gives us different tasks every six weeks. It helps. I'll be sorry when I have to leave."

"Maybe he should try again, but with a different tack this time. See if he could find an older teacher who is about to retire, who would love to spend the next couple of years in this setting."

"That's a good idea; why don't you suggest it to Dane?" Lisa said.

Mary-Kate didn't think he'd take kindly to any idea from her, but she only nodded, not wanting to have to explain anything to Lisa. If the opportunity came up before she left she would, otherwise she'd write to Lisa and tell her she hadn't been able to do so, and urge her to talk to Dane.

"The sun makes me so sleepy," Lisa said, lying back on the towel, pushing her glasses firmly in place. "I'll just doze for a few minutes."

"Don't get burned," Mary-Kate warned from experience, though Lisa was so brown that she probably had no worry about burning.

"I know, I've got sunscreen on . . ." Her voice trailed off.

Mary-Kate sat back and watched the surfers, fascinated, as they gracefully rose up on the boards and balanced on the moving water. The waves looked large to her, but not as high as she knew they got in winter. She'd heard that they could get up to twenty feet or more. It would frighten her to challenge waves that size. Yet Dane had said those were the best. He obviously relished the challenge.

Her eyes sought him out, spotted him as he lithely rose up on his board and began skimming along a wall of water just below the crest of the wave, cutting at an angle, always ahead of the froth as the wave curled over, until, unable to stay ahead, he was enclosed by the curl and the wave boomed on the beach, its spray thrown high into the sunshine. She watched, breath held, until she saw him pushing back out for the next one.

He was poetry and grace in motion, his body balanced on the board, riding each wave he took from the first swell to the last froth of white water. As he swam back for the next one, Mary-Kate realized why his chest and shoulder muscles were so developed. He'd probably been surfing since he was a child.

Mary-Kate grew hotter and hotter as she sat in the sun. The wind from the water was strong, but hot. Lisa was asleep, so Mary-Kate decided to take a quick swim to cool off. She looked up and down the beach, and saw a deserted area to her right. Waves peaked and crashed there, but it was out of the line of the surfers. There were no swimmers, either, but Mary-Kate wasn't concerned. She wouldn't go out far, and would be in plain sight of shore.

Dropping her hat and cover-up, she walked to the water's edge and along the firm sand. The water was cool on her hot feet and ankles. It would cool her entire body when she plunged in. The sea tugged at her as if imploring her to come in, to give herself up to its coolness. She waded out and dived through an incoming wave, the water cool and refreshing. Clearing the wave, she swam out a little more, flipping on her back. It was delightful. She would remember this vacation all her life. Next winter, when she sat before her fire, she would remember the warm beach, the fragrant air and the vivid colors of the islands.

She turned over, glanced to shore, a touch of concern hitting her when she saw how far out she was. She began swimming in. It was like swimming upstream in a fast-moving river. Mary-Kate tried harder, her arms cutting deep into the water, her legs beating hard against it.

Her concern turned to fear. She was alone, far from the beach, and wasn't getting any closer. The swells rushing to shore only raised her up to glimpse the sandy strip so far away, but they did not carry her closer. She struck off at an angle to see if it would take her closer. It did not.

Panic coursed through her when a small wave splashed down on her, filling her mouth and nose with stinging salt water. What if she couldn't make it back? She was growing tired, her arms and legs heavy, ineffectively beating the water. She trod water while she coughed out the salt water. Then started again. Her arms ached with tiredness, her legs kicked each other almost as much as they kicked the water. She was growing weaker. The shore was further away than ever. Was she just to float away?

"Mary-Kate!" The voice was familiar.

She stopped swimming and looked around. To her right, seemingly miles away, she saw Dane, lying on his surfboard, his powerful arms propelling him along the top of the water. He was coming toward her. Relief washed through her.

"Swim toward me!" he called.

She trod water for another minute to catch her breath, to get some strength back into her body, then she started again, forcing her arms to move, kicking with dead legs. Dane skimmed along the surface, and in only minutes was beside her. He sat up, straddling the board, and reached over to pull her up before him on it.

Mary-Kate was tired and scared. Thankfully she leaned back against the hard, solid strength of his chest, gasping for air, her muscles trembling in exhaustion.

"Now what damn-fool stunt were you trying?" he growled in her ear, as his arm drew her back against him. The heat of his body on her back and the tight band of his arm beneath her breasts penetrated the cold chill of fear. Mary-Kate relaxed fractionally.

"I...I just wanted to go swimming." She burst into tears.

His arm tightened. "Well, you picked one damnable spot to do it. That's the worst riptide on the island. Didn't you see the sign?"

She dashed the tears away, and shook her head, feeling like a complete fool. "I walked along the beach and it was the one area that was deserted—no surfers, no swimmers, so I thought it would be a good spot.''

She tried to sit up, to pull away from Dane's disturbing body, but his arms tightened as the surfboard wobbled slightly, then settled down to bob quietly on the water. She was conscious of his legs on either side of hers, the strength of his body behind her, the heat from his skin. Warmth rose within her. The amount of clothing between them would hardly make a good-size handkerchief.

Dane's legs were muscular and brown, straddling the board, cradling hers. Her hips back against his, she stared off into the vast emptiness of the Pacific, feeling closed in and protected. His arm around her was heavy, his chest hard, secure and warm. She wanted to turn in his arms, press her scantily clad body against his, feel the heat of his skin on hers.

Mary-Kate leaned her head back against his shoulder, feeling his muscles tighten. The surfboard floated gently on the sea, riding the swells, quiet and still. She closed her eyes, safe and content in Dane's arms.

''Do you propose to go to sleep?'' his mocking voice asked softly. His fingers gently rubbed the soft skin on her ribs, his thumb skimmed the swell of her breast.

She opened her eyes, turning her head to see him. His tan was darker for the time in the sun, his eyes silvery and soft, his hair light in the sun.

"Thank you for rescuing me. I was so scared. Now I feel safe."

"I wouldn't, if I were you." His voice was low, and he turned her slightly, his lips capturing hers in a cool kiss, as his hand covered one breast.

Mary-Kate was startled into acquiescence, then sanity returned. They were in plain sight of dozens of people on the shore. She struggled to pull free, upsetting the balance on the board. Dane pulled away at the last second, tried to stabilize the board, but was too late. They both spilled into the water.

Mary-Kate debated remaining beneath the shimmery sea forever, but knew she couldn't. Slowly she broke the surface, nervously searching for Dane. He clung to the board, a big grin on his face as she swam the short distance to him.

"No kiss?" he teased.

"We are in front of half the people on the island! I thought you were reluctant for talk." She avoided his eyes, wondering how they would get back on the board.

"That the only reason?"

She refused to meet his eyes. "Are we going to be able to get back on the board?"

He chuckled at her obvious tactics, and effortlessly vaulted onto the board.

"I'm on; how are you getting on?"

"Can't you pull me up again?" She met his eyes, which was a mistake. Her heart began hammering in her chest and her muscles grew weaker. Involuntarily her gaze dropped to his lips.

He leaned over, dangerously close. "I can, but it will cost you a kiss," he said softly, wickedly.

She looked to the shore; it was too far for her to swim back. Biting her lip in indecision, she looked up at him again from beneath her lashes. Why was she hesitating? She liked his kisses. Not that they meant anything. He had made that perfectly clear. But she had to get back.

She nodded, afraid to speak.

He chuckled again, his eyes laughing at her. Reaching down, he easily drew her onto the board again, but this time he made her sit sideways, and he drew her against him for his kiss. Mary-Kate had been cool from the sea, but when her breasts were crushed to his chest she instantly grew warm. His lips moved over hers, tasting her, moving to open her lips for access to her mouth. His tongue was hot and exciting as he traced the softness of her lips, dueled with her tongue.

She clung to him in wild abandonment, reveling in his touch. His left arm held her against him while his right hand wandered across her skin, inflaming it, negating the cooling effect of the sea. He moved to her side, to her breasts, slipping beneath the skimpy material that covered her. His fingers entrapped her nipple, tugging gently, bringing it to aching awareness of his touch.

"I've been wanting to touch you for ages," he murmured against her lips.

She moaned softly, her body on fire, yearnings for fulfilment engulfing her. It was heavenly madness. It must stop. She struggled to sit up, reluctantly pulling away when he let her. Searching his eyes for some sign, she saw nothing but the silvery gray. He turned his head and looked toward the beach.

Mary-Kate moved cautiously, startled when Dane encircled her waist and moved her exactly where he wanted her, before him, her back to him. "Are we all right? Can we make it back?" The distance looked formidable.

"Sure." His answer was casual, confident.

Mary-Kate looked at Dane again. He was calm, totally in control of himself and her fate. He acted as if the kiss had caused no reaction, had meant nothing. Yet she was shaken to her soul. Tears blurred her vision and she turned away, never letting him see how she felt.

He knew the islands, the sea. If he thought they'd make it back safely, then they would. He reached into the water, and turned the board toward shore. "We'll bypass the riptide and shoot in on a wave."

Before Mary-Kate could say anything, he slipped off the back of the board, kicking to propel it shoreward.

"What should I do?" she asked, the board wobbly with his kicks.

"Get your feet out of the water; they're excess drag. Otherwise, just hang on and enjoy the ride!"

And Mary-Kate did. Gradually the beach drew nearer. She could distinguish the different people she'd met. The surfers were close now, sitting on their boards, some watching them, others watching for the next perfect wave. She could hear the surf crashing on the shore, muffled a little from the distance.

The board sank a little, then tipped back as Dane vaulted on again, cool water washing over the surface. Mary-Kate didn't think the surfboard was big enough to move around on, and she held on to the edges tightly.

"Okay, Mary-Kate; next big wave, we'll ride it in." Dane's voice was calm.

"I don't know how to surf," she nervously reminded him.

"All you have to do is stand up when I tell you to, and lean against me, sway with me, move when I do. I'll hold you. Ready?"

"I can't do this." Her eyes darted here and there, frantically looking for another way.

"Sure you can. Get up on your knees—easy, now." His hands steadied her as she got to her knees, balancing carefully so not to fall over. She could feel the wave build beneath the board, swelling, rising.

Dane maneuvered the board with his hands, angling it ahead of the wave, then suddenly he stood, pulled Mary-Kate upright, and held her tightly against him.

"Relax. Keep the board beneath you. Move when I move. Easy."

They caught the wave and were away on a thrill ride, better than anything she'd ridden at Six

Flags. The sea hissed beneath the board, the threatening rumble of the crest chased them as Dane cut diagonally across the face, heading for the shore at lightning speed.

Mary-Kate could almost touch the wall of water as it built on her right, while the left side dropped into a trough, the bottom of which she could not see. She looked up; the board continued its race toward shore, always at an angle to the beach. The wind blew her hair back, the mist from the wave captured the sunlight and blazed a rainbow of blinding intensity with a million fragmented droplets.

It was terrifying, terrific, frightening and fascinating. She could scarcely take it all in. She gave herself up to the enjoyment of the ride, trusting in the ability of the man holding her to keep her safe. She could feel him moving, constantly adjusting the board, shifting their weight from side to side, compensating for her.

"Hold on—it's catching us," Dane shouted in her ear. The world tilted, and they were plunged into the swirling water, churning and turning as the wave finished its crash on the shore. Mary-Kate caught her breath before going under, instinctively turning to shore, moving with the force of the wave.

When she felt the firm sand beneath her, she struggled to her feet. She was still waist deep in swirling frothy water, and staggered toward shore against the outward pull.

Dane was a few yards to her right, pulling in his board. He searched for her, moving toward her when he saw her. "You all right?" he asked.

"That was great! Thank you!" she exclaimed, exhilarated by the ride, by the day's beauty—and by Dane Carmichael.

"Stay away from the rip; next time we might not be so lucky," he said, but he didn't seem angry. His eyes were light and sparkling.

Several of the other surfers rode in on the next wave, stopping near Dane. In only a moment he was surrounded.

"Some trick, man! You took a chance."

"You okay, boss? You were a long way out..."

"Thought we were going to have to go for the launch."

From those remarks, and others that were called out, Mary-Kate realized she'd been right to be scared. They had been in danger. But Dane had made it seem so safe, so ordinary.

On shore Marco and Rames were running up and down at the water's edge, barking. They would stop just short of plunging in, tearing back and forth, tails wagging, anxious to see their master.

She watched as the men and women crowded around Dane. He was well liked, it was obvious. They were concerned for her, too. Complimenting her on her first ride, again warning her about the dangers of the riptide. When Dane headed back to the sea, Mary-Kate turned and walked over the burning sand to drop down by

Lisa. The dogs trotted patiently along at her side, running off along the sand once she was seated.

"You okay?" Lisa asked.

"I am now; I was scared for a while, though."

"Sorry I went to sleep. I could have told you about the rip. There's a sign on the beach—not that we need it; we all know about it. Treacherous."

Mary-Kate shivered despite the heat. "It was."

She donned her hat and settled down to watch the surfers. In the future, she'd swim in the cove beneath the house, leave the big waves to the group on the boards.

The future? She didn't have a future here. Either the Lombards would return, or the supply ship would carry her away. Dane would do nothing to stop her, would actually be glad to see her go.

And she'd be glad to go. She had nothing to do on the island. Though she thought there could be work for her here. But Dane had said nothing, and any time she brought it up he got angry. He did not want her to stay. She would be fine for a casual fling while she awaited the supply ship, but that was all. He'd been very clear.

Some of her enjoyment of the day was dampened. She lay back, idly thinking of some of the changes she'd make, if she were staying.

It was late afternoon when Dane rode his last wave in, all the way to shore. He drew up his surfboard and hoisted it under his arm. Walking quickly on the hot sand, he made his way to Mary-Kate.

"Ready to go?" he asked.

"Sure." She averted her eyes from the strong figure before her, his skin glistening in the sun, water still dripping. She was glad for the excuse to gather her towel, check for her sunscreen, and bid Lisa goodbye.

"Oh, you'll be seeing me again, I'm sure," Lisa said in a friendly manner.

Mary-Kate smiled as she walked across the hot sand to the jeep. She liked Lisa; she felt she'd made a friend on the island. Maybe they could visit each other a couple of times before Mary-Kate caught the supply boat. Dane whistled for the dogs, and they came running. Sand flew everywhere as they bounded into the jeep.

As they drove across the island, Mary-Kate again brought up the subject of her departure. She was enjoying herself, maybe too much. If she didn't go soon, she wouldn't want to go at all.

"Dane, one of the guys mentioned a launch. Could that take me to one of the other islands?"

He said nothing at first, but she noticed that his jaw clenched. Finally he answered, "No, it's too far, and the launch couldn't make it. This is our busiest time, and I need everyone working, so couldn't spare anyone to take you even if the launch were a long-distance boat. I know you can't wait to get out of here, but you're going to have to wait for the supply boat. Can't you keep yourself amused for a few days?'' His voice was curiously bitter and bewildered.

"That's easy for you to say; you have your work, your friends. I'm not the type to lie around the beach all day and stare at the water.''

"Work doesn't solve everything. I've had dozen of workers who can't stick it. Nothing to do in the way of entertainment is the most common reason given for not staying.''

Mary-Kate thought of what Lisa had said about the teachers. "Maybe you should recruit older people—ones who are more settled, who don't want crowds and excitement and constant action.''

"Maybe.''

"Though, from what I saw today, most of the people on the beach love it here.''

"Yes, but, even so, there's talk of leaving.''

"Because of schooling for their kids.''

"Right.''

"But I would think you'd be able to get a good teacher to handle it; it's just a matter of finding the right one,'' she said reasonably.

"You want the job?''

For a long moment Mary-Kate considered it. It would be far different from her high school in Ames. More like schoolteachers of old: one room, various ages. A challenge to teach them all, hold their interest, impart knowledge.

She stole a quick glance at Dane, her heart beating faster. She couldn't stay. She was growing too interested in the man beside her. It would be safer to go back to the life she'd always known. Not make a fool of herself the way the other teachers had. Not fall in love with the unattainable Dane Carmichael.

She only hoped it wasn't too late.

Slowly, regretfully, she shook her head. "I don't think I'd be the right one."

"I don't think so, either."

He was silent for the rest of the trip.

CHAPTER SEVEN

DANE pulled the jeep to a stop near the veranda, turned off the motor, and turned to look at Mary-Kate. She met his eyes hesitantly, questioningly.

"Thank you for taking me. And for saving me in the sea."

"Again."

"Again?"

"Saving you again. You need a keeper."

"I do not!"

"Sure you do; you go on a boat, and get left behind. You sunbathe, and get burned. You try swimming, and almost drown! You obviously need a keeper. Life must be more dangerous here in Hawaii than in Iowa."

"And I think you're the most dangerous part of all," she said softly, her eyes dropping to his mouth.

"Damn right!" His hand encircled her neck, slowly pulling her toward him while his head dropped until his lips were inches away. His warm breath fanned her face, mingled with her own, as her eyes widened first in startled surprise, then narrowed as she shook her head.

He ignored her protest, his warm mouth covering hers. Mary-Kate hesitated, remaining rigid, unyielding for a moment, then capitulated.

She moved fractionally closer, and moved her lips beneath his. His free hand moved beneath her cover-up to caress the skin beneath her breasts. Mary-Kate was lost.

She moved closer, her hands finding their way to the strong muscles of his chest, tracing the hot skin, the smooth muscles that gave strength to his arms. She moved to his neck, to the thickness of his hair. Moving even closer, she opened her mouth to his demands. While his tongue learned the sweet secrets of her mouth, she learned what a man's touch could do to her, what pleasure and delight it could cause. But it was not enough.

Never mind that he didn't trust her, never mind that he didn't believe her story about being left behind. She didn't care. All she wanted was for this moment to go on endlessly.

When his hand cupped her breast, pushing aside the scrap of pink that covered it, Mary-Kate shivered and drew back. "Dane, please; Nora——"

"Nora's at the compound. Everyone's at the compound. There's no one within a mile of this place." His hand fondled her breast, feeling it swell to his touch, the nipple hardening to a thrusting peak. "There's no one here but you and me." His voice was low and seductive. He moved to kiss the slope of her breast, to capture its saucy peak in his mouth, suckle gently, rasping its tip with his hot tongue.

Mary-Kate moaned; she was thrilled, and scared, wanting more, knowing she must stop now if she was ever to stop. But for another long moment she let Dane kiss her, bring her to the edge of rapture.

"Dane, stop; I can't let you seduce me." She pushed against his shoulders, closing her eyes against the pain she felt as he pulled back.

His laugh was as unexpected as it was harsh.

"Me, seduce you? Sweetheart, I thought *you* were seducing *me*!" his voice mocked, his eyes glittering down at her.

"Well, I wasn't." She wasn't leading him on. She wasn't a tease, as he'd said once before. He kissed her. He started it. But you didn't resist. Not at first, her conscience said.

He sat back and watched her from brooding eyes, his hand still at her waist, gently massaging her hot skin. Mary-Kate could scarcely breathe. She didn't want him to stop, but he had to, or they'd be back where they were a moment ago, and this time she might not say no.

A long black nose poked over the seat from the back; Marco whined at still being confined in the car. Startled by the interruption, Dane swore softly and opened the door, motioning the dogs to get out. They took off without further invitation.

Mary-Kate reached for his hand, pulled it slowly away, her eyes wide as she tried to keep the tears that welled from falling. She felt such a fool. Why could other women gracefully get out of situations like this, while she acted like a scared fifteen-year-old?

"There's a barbecue at the compound; that's where Nora is. Everyone's eating together to-night. Want to go?" He stared out of the wind-shield, his face impassive.

She nodded. Anything was preferable to being alone for the next few hours. And she dared not trust herself around him.

"I'll give you a head start on the shower. Be ready in half an hour."

Mary-Kate scrambled from the jeep, and fled to the house, her breathing constricted, her eyes blurred with unshed tears. She closed the door to her bedroom, and raced for the shower. Once beneath its warm water, she let the tears flow.

You're such a fool! Why can't you play the same game? Or at least be sophisticated when refusing? Damn everything! He probably thinks I'm the biggest prude in America, she berated herself.

How could she explain to him that she be-lieved in love and fidelity—that she wasn't interested in casual sex, no matter how ap-pealing? She wanted someone who loved her, whom she could love.

And she could love Dane Carmichael. She felt the strong attraction when she was around him. She thought of him constantly when they were apart. But he had made it very clear that he was not interested in anything permanent. And she was not interested in anything temporary.

Stalemate.

She'd go to dinner, and enjoy herself. She would take pleasure in all the different aspects of the island, storing up memories for the days ahead when she would never see it again.

Mary-Kate was pleased to be at the jeep before Dane. At least he could not complain about her promptness. The sun was sinking toward the west, and the breeze from the water had picked up. She wondered if she'd be cold later, but it couldn't be helped—she had nothing to use as a wrap.

When Dane joined her a few moments later, he nodded and climbed into the jeep. Gone was the would-be lover of earlier. Back was the scowling plantation owner.

Maybe it was better that way, she thought as they started off. Safer for her, anyway.

The barbecue was in full swing when they arrived. Makeshift picnic tables with wooden benches encircled the large yard before the processing plant, and colorful lanterns were strung around, providing illumination. There was a huge barbecue pit and several tables laden with food.

Many faces were familiar to Mary-Kate when she walked to the food tables. She smiled at those she recognized, calling a greeting, hoping she wouldn't be called on to remember their names.

Lisa waved to her and motioned her to join them. Mary-Kate chose her food and walked across to her new friend. She sat on the bench opposite Lisa, and smiled at her. Seconds later,

Dane's plate was placed beside hers, and he slipped into the bench.

"How you feeling, Lisa?" he asked without a glance at Mary-Kate.

"Great. Morning sickness is gone, and I feel wonderful." She glanced thoughtfully at Dane and Mary-Kate and then back at her food. "Mike will be along in a minute. He was checking something at the plant. Surfing good today?"

"For summer."

"Mary-Kate, how did you like it?" Lisa's smile was friendly.

Dane's leg rubbed against Mary-Kate, startling her, causing her heartbeat to increase, her concentration to vanish. She was overwhelmingly aware of the man sitting only inches from her, the crisp hair of his legs rasping against her silky skin.

She swallowed hard, and looked at Lisa. Apparently the other woman saw nothing amiss; she was politely awaiting Mary-Kate's response. "I think I'd rather be a spectator to the sport than actually do it. It was rather frightening."

"But fun, too," Dane murmured at her side.

She darted a quick glance at him, and it was her undoing. His eyes twinkled down at her; he knew what his touch was doing, and was amused by her reaction.

Anger flared within Mary-Kate. She was not some toy for him to play with.

"Fun, but overrated—like some other things I can think of," she retorted, glaring at him.

Dane chuckled and turned back to his food. His leg didn't move, however, and Mary-Kate was loath to be the first to give way. She tilted her head; she would not give him the satisfaction. Two would play this game!

Mike joined them, and another couple—Roy and Joyce. Mary-Kate was glad of the opportunity to thank Joyce in person for the loan of her clothes, and the conversation remained general while they ate.

For Mary-Kate it was the longest meal she'd ever eaten. She felt split in two—one part of her concentrating on the conversation that flowed around the table, contributing where she could, asking questions about things she didn't know. The other part of her, however, was focused on Dane. His every movement caused her blood to surge, her heartbeat to change rhythm. When his hands picked up the mango and held it a moment before biting into it, she remembered his hands on her that afternoon, on the surfboard, in the jeep. When his mouth bit into the fruit she remembered the touch of his lips on her skin, the feel of his mouth enveloping her when he'd kissed her breast, when his tongue had invaded her mouth and brought her to the edge of rapture.

When Roy suggested that he procure coffee for the table, Mary-Kate breathed a sigh of relief. She had proved her point; she could now move, and show Dane Carmichael that he had no effect on her. Gracefully she shifted positions on the bench, moving away from his disturbing touch, gaining a moment's respite against the assault on her senses that his touch, his very nearness, wrought.

Soft Hawaiian music played in the background. Conversations around the compound gradually died, and everyone watched as one of the girls stepped into the open and began a lovely, graceful hula.

As Mary-Kate turned on the bench to see better, Dane turned also, his arm coming around her shoulders. She stiffened for a moment, but, when she made to protest, his attention was on the lovely dancer before them.

Mary-Kate watched the young girl as she moved through the motions of the song. Her hips gently swayed from side to side, and her feet stepped to the beat of the music as her arms made lovely motions before her.

"Do you know how to interpret the hula?" Dane's soft voice asked in her ear.

Mary-Kate shook her head, eyes on the dancer.

"She's alone . . . working . . . The house she has is sad, for it is empty . . . A man comes to woo her, but when he discovers she is poor he leaves . . . No others come to woo her, and she is alone . . . A big storm comes, and the waves crash on the beach, and she is frightened—alone and frightened . . . When the storm passes, the day is beautiful . . . She walks along the shore . . . and finds the body of a sailor . . . She nurses him to health . . . and he leaves . . . and she is alone, but not sad, because she has found love with the sailor... A long time passes... then the sailor returns, with many presents, and with desire to stay with the girl... She is no longer alone... she is loved.''

Mary-Kate was enchanted. The pantomime of the song was clear as Dane explained it. The melody was haunting, the theme sad, until the end. Everyone applauded, and the young girl flushed with pride and happiness, bowing to her friends.

"I bet all tourists who see the hula want to learn it." Mary-Kate turned to Dane, her comment forgotten when she saw how close they were. His lips were only inches from hers, and his eyes were disturbing as they gazed down at her in the light of the lanterns.

"Of course. Hawaii is romance; that's why people come here, isn't it?''

She nodded, unable to look away, uncaring what the others at the table might think, what Dane might be thinking. She only wanted to go on looking into his silvery eyes until daylight.

The music changed, and people moved to the center space to dance. Dane didn't ask Mary-Kate; he simply took her hand and led her to the clearing. The tempo was slow, and he drew her into his arms, wrapping his around her, and they moved together to the sweet melody.

One hand was at her spine, the other on her hip, where it flared. He drew her against him. Her soft breasts flattened against the strength of his chest, then swelled with longing and desire.

Her body was pressed hard against his, feeling his muscles move as they swayed and danced. She could feel his desire for her, and she looked up into his knowing eyes in startled awareness.

His mouth found hers and took it in a kiss, passionate, hot and pulsating, in sharp contrast to the dreamy music they swayed to. Mary-Kate moved against him, instinctively moving closer, her hips moving in tempo with the music, her heart beating against his. She was floating on a sea of delight, an endless time of enchantment, lost to the world as she knew it, alive only to feelings and emotions never before experienced.

The music stopped. It was several seconds before Dane released her, and drew back, his eyes never leaving hers.

"Break it up, you two, or you'll start talk," Mike jokingly broke in. "Dane, you got a thing for schoolteachers?"

Mary-Kate flushed in embarrassment and looked away, knowing Dane would be furious now, and would withdraw and be impossible to be around. Another song was starting, with a fast beat, and Mike asked Mary-Kate if she'd care to dance with him, since Lisa preferred to sit out the fast ones.

Smiling at the man for his intervention, she nodded and moved out, ignoring Dane. She did not want to be the latest in the line of schoolteachers who had tried to ensnare the man.

Halfway through the dance, Mary-Kate glanced around, and found Dane sitting beside

Lisa; but his eyes were on her. She danced with several of the young men over the next few hours, but only to the fast songs. When the next slow song started, Mary-Kate turned to her last partner, only to find Dane before her.

He drew her into his arms, and passion flared. Mary-Kate took a deep breath, and tried to talk calmly, to keep her emotions at bay. "Don't you dance fast ones?"

"Sure, but why not give the other guys a chance? You'll notice the men outnumber the women by quite a bit."

"Maybe I should be dancing this with someone else?"

"No; I don't want anyone else taking you in his arms. Do you?" Dane looked down at her, his face in shadow, hers illuminated by the fire.

She looked away. In truth, she didn't want to dance any of the dances with anyone but Dane, and she didn't want to be anywhere but where he was. To be in his arms was to be in heaven.

He didn't pursue it, only drew her closer, burying his face in her soft curls. She relaxed and gave herself up to the enjoyment of the moment.

Twice more, when the songs were slow, Dane claimed her. The rest of the time, he seemed content to let her do what she wanted; but his eyes never left her. She wondered what he was thinking as she danced with the other men, broke off into small groups, chatting with the friendly island people. It was a good party. Was Dane also enjoying it?

It was late when people began leaving, late when Dane found her with a small group of mothers, discussing day-camp programs for young children. The topic was interesting, and she felt the frustration of the young mothers because there was nothing for their children.

The ride to the house was quiet, Mary-Kate thinking about the party, remembering the dances with Dane. Would he try to kiss her when they reached the house? Would he be content to stop with only kisses? Could she provide anything more?

The closer they got, the more nervous Mary-Kate became. She wasn't ready for anything. She only wanted to be left alone. In only a few days, the island boat would come, and she would be on her way back to the life she knew—the life she'd loved before coming here. She wasn't into summer romances.

When he stopped the jeep, she quickly fumbled for her seat belt, wanting to escape to the safety of her room. His hand stopped her, unfastened her belt, and held her hand in his.

"You're not playing your cards right, sweetheart," he murmured.

Mary-Kate did not want to get into a duel of wits with him tonight. Her emotional state was too precarious. Without much more incentive, she'd throw caution to the winds and take whatever he offered.

"Thanks for taking me to the barbecue. And for the dances..." Her voice trailed off to a whisper.

"I can't figure you out." Dane's voice was puzzled.

"I know; I can't either," she said, giving him a fleeting kiss at the edge of his mouth and scrambling out of the jeep.

"Mary-Kate?" His voice followed her as she sought the safe darkness of her room. She closed the door, and undressed in the dark, not wanting to give any invitation to the man on the other side.

CHAPTER EIGHT

THE droning of a small plane woke Mary-Kate the next morning. Idly she sought it through the window, its white and blue markings bright in the clear morning sky. It was the first airplane she'd seen in a long time, and she wondered where it was from and where it was going. It was flying low, so it was probably a sight-seeing plane from Lanai.

For one mad moment, Mary-Kate considered dashing out on the patio and waving to the plane, signaling her need for help. But the pilot would only think she was being friendly. Who would imagine she wanted to be rescued from such a paradise? Besides, she smiled to herself, where would he land, in the pineapple fields? Wouldn't Dane just love that!

Time to get up.

Mary-Kate ate a solitary breakfast, Dane having already gone for the day, as Nora informed her. She didn't know whether to be relieved or not. After yesterday, she wanted some time to herself to sort out her feelings, clamp down on runaway emotions.

On the other hand, she wished she could see him. The days were slipping away as the date of the supply ship's arrival drew nearer. And at any time the Lombards could return. Though Mary-Kate was finding that more unlikely as each day passed. She shook her head at their lack of concern for her safety. What if this had been a deserted island? Or if Dane had refused any help?

She lingered over breakfast, but, after that, what? Mary-Kate was bored. During school, she taught, tutored slower students, assisted the drama teacher in the school productions. She had a wide assortment of friends in Ames, and usually found someone to go shopping with, or see a movie, or go out to dinner.

Even on the Lombard yacht, she had had things to do, people to talk to, although she had spent most of the time avoiding the more amorous friends of Rob Lombard.

She took stock. She had no watch, no clothes—except those borrowed—no money, no credit cards. When the supply boat came, she'd have to have money. It would cost something for her passage. Once she reached the other islands, it might be a day or two before her family could send her funds, or before she found the Lombards' yacht. She would need money.

With the glimmer of an idea, Mary-Kate got up from the table and sought Dane's study. She was too impatient to wait to talk to Dane about her idea; she wanted to work on it, formulate it, have it in place before telling him.

The morning swiftly passed. After lunch, she walked to the compound. It was hot and dusty, but Mary-Kate didn't notice today; she was still planning.

The activity in the area was bustling. The trucks continued to roll in, loaded with freshly picked fruit. Mary-Kate stepped wide of the trucks, not wanting a repeat of her last visit. She searched among the working men, looking for Dane. He'd be easy to spot; he was the tallest of the men, stood out from the others. Her heart beat faster in anticipation. Would he like her idea, go along with her? Or scoff at it, seeing it as only another ploy to gain his attention?

She was disappointed when she didn't see him. "Hi, Mary-Kate." She smiled in recognition at Mike. He'd know where Dane was. "Here to work today?"

She walked over to him. "Don't think Dane wants me to; I've asked. No surfing today?"

"Might take off early if the wind picks up again."

"I'm looking for Dane."

"Not here."

One of the trucks pulled out, its engine loud. When it passed, Mike grinned, and nodded to the north. "Might be at the point—Halikia Point—north end of the island."

Mary-Kate was still disappointed, but not deterred. "How about Lisa; is she around?"

"Sure." He walked to the large open doors of the plant, and pointed Lisa out. "Second row, facing us."

Mary-Kate saw her, and threaded her way through boxes and people, wondering if she could speak with her for a few minutes about her idea.

Lisa looked up and smiled. "Hi; want to pack some pineapple?"

"Not today, thanks. Actually I have another idea. When you can take a break, I'd like to hear what you think about it."

"Give me ten minutes," Lisa said, glancing at the clock.

Mary-Kate watched the women deftly stack the sliced pineapple into cans. The conveyor belts deposited them at the end, where sturdy men stacked them in racks and pushed them to the topping machine. The air was saturated with pineapple, its sweet scent causing Mary-Kate's mouth to water. She wished she could take one of them as they came through, and eat it while she waited.

At last, Lisa threw down her knife and stood up, stretching before turning to Mary-Kate. "Let's get some fresh air. I get so sick of the pineapple."

When they were settled on the porch of Lisa's small cottage, Mary-Kate broached the subject of her morning's work.

"I'd like to have a day camp for the kids for as long as I'm here. I'd have organized activities, teach a little, and take them off their mothers' hands. Let the women work more hours at the plant, if that's what they want. Or just relax without the children under foot."

"I think it would be grand. There's a wide assortment of ages, though," Lisa reminded her.

"I thought of that. But for summer activities, I don't think it would matter. The older kids can help with the younger ones. We can all enjoy some of the same things, like swimming at the beach, or collecting shells. They could make gifts for people from the shells. Dane's got a ton of books about the islands, the flowers, and other plants. We could have lessons that the kids wouldn't even know were lessons."

"I like it. Want to talk it over with Joyce and Mary? They were talking about it last night."

"That's what gave me the idea. I wish I could do it until school starts, but I have to go when the supply boat comes. But that should still be a couple of weeks away, and it will be something different for the kids."

The mothers whom Mary-Kate discussed it with were delighted with the idea. It would give them extra time to work, and the money Mary-Kate agreed to take was low. But it would give her something to do, and enough money to get to one of the other islands until her family could send her money.

She was keyed up and excited, spending the entire afternoon doing plans for the next day. She wanted to tell Dane, share her idea with him, and get his approval, but he had not returned by the time she went to bed.

Mary-Kate arose early the next morning, excited about her first day with the children. She ate a hasty breakfast, and headed for the compound, in one hand a sheaf of papers with the games and plans she'd made, in the other, her lunch.

Overhead a small blue and white plane droned. Mary-Kate looked up; was it the same one as yesterday? Was this a new route on the sight-seeing itinerary? If it was passing regularly, maybe she could devise some signal, some way to notify the pilot that she needed to contact people on the mainland.

With a pang, Mary-Kate dropped her eyes. She was torn. She knew she had to leave, and before long. Yet she didn't want to say goodbye to Dane. Not just yet. She'd never have a reason to come this way again. When she left, it would be forever. No, she'd not send a message to the pilot; she'd stay until the supply boat arrived. Time enough then to say goodbye.

The day passed swiftly. The children were eager and excited about the plans she'd made. Enthusiastically they joined in the projects she outlined, and Mary-Kate found that the day flew by.

As she trudged back to the house in the late afternoon, tired, but happy, she planned what she'd do tomorrow. A quiet glow of pride pervaded her; it had gone well. The children were well-behaved and pleasant to be around. The activities she'd planned had pleased the children, and both she and the children had been disappointed when the day had come to an end.

They were smart, too. She'd have to work hard to stay ahead of them, keep their interest and attention. And their enthusiasm. But she loved the challenge. It was different from high-school algebra, but just as rewarding.

Mary-Kate wandered out to the veranda after she'd showered and changed for dinner. Dane was sitting on one of the chairs, a large pitcher of pineapple juice and two glasses beside him. She smiled, gladness swelling within her. She was anxious to share the news of her new job with him, hoping he'd be pleased she had found something to do.

"If one of those glasses is for me, I'll not say no," she said as she sat down in the chair near him.

He poured the fresh juice into the glasses, and lightly touched his rim to hers.

"You look like the cat that swallowed the canary," he commented as he took a sip.

"I am." She tossed her head proudly and beamed at him. "I got a job."

He sat up, startled, his eyes narrowed. "Where, doing what?"

"Here on the island, running a summer camp for the children."

He watched her for a few moments, and then a sardonic smile settled on his features. Leaning back, he raised his glass to her again. "Clever. Very clever."

Mary-Kate was puzzled; why that word? A little of her happiness dimmed. Her smile faded. He didn't like the idea.

"Show us all how indispensable you are, and we'll keep you forever," he murmured sarcastically.

"Oh, shut up! I was bored. You work all day, everyone else on this island works all day. But there's nothing for me to do. I can only read so much. I can't stare off into space for hours on end. Could you? At the dinner the other night, several mothers were talking about the problem of keeping their kids busy during the summer, and how they could earn some more money during the busy time, if they didn't have to watch the kids. I came up with a plan that helps everyone out, and gets me some money so that when I leave I can pay my way."

"I would arrange that."

"I don't need you to do that."

"A good ploy, but you'll grow tired of it soon. Reality is far different from pipe dreams." He looked out across the ocean, his lips tight, his eyes narrowed.

Mary-Kate looked closely at him. Was he angry?

"What ploy? I think it's a great idea, and I've already spent the day with the kids. It's working out fine."

"But it won't last," he said flatly. "I know women; they want what money can get them, that's all. Look at my mother; she's on her sixth husband, or is it seventh? Always wanting more, wanting to do more. She's doing Europe again. Not satisfied with the life my father could have given her; no, she wants to be off, jetting around, spending money, having a good time." His voice was bitter.

"Dane..."

"Melissa, the same way. She finds out how much money I make, and she immediately wants to install a manager and take off for San Francisco. We could stop back here from time to time to make sure everything was running smoothly, she graciously consented."

He sat up, carefully placing his glass on the table, his eyes boring into Mary-Kate's. "Who are you really, Mary-Kate O'Donnell? Why are you here to disrupt my life? To show me what's missing, what I'll never have?" His eyes glinted in the late sun.

"I'm not disrupting anyone's life! I was stranded here—ditched, dumped, and am stuck here until I can get off. I'm trying to make the most of a bad situation. This makes everything fine. I can enjoy the island, yet have some purpose."

"You seem content with the life of the islands, but how soon before you long for the excitement of the city, the variety of the stores, long for plays and nightclubs and parties?" His hands gripped the arms of her chair.

"Not me—you have me confused with the other women you hang out with!" Mary-Kate leaned forward, her face only inches from Dane's. "I like a good time, but I wouldn't miss night-clubs—I never go to them in Iowa. Shopping is fine, but once in a while is plenty. Friends are important to me, and I like staying home and visiting."

"It's easy to say now, but how would you feel after several weeks here, or several months?"

"I won't be here that long, remember? I'm leaving on the supply boat when it comes." She wished it weren't so, but better that it was. She needed to get away, while she still could. And it was obvious he wanted her gone.

"I remember! And it can't come too soon!" His words were harsh.

Nora came to the door. "Dinner's ready; you want to eat out there?"

"No, we'll come in." Dane shoved back his chair, and turned for the house, pausing at the door, waiting with unconcealed impatience for Mary-Kate to precede him.

"Heard about your summer camp, missy," Nora said as she dished up the broiled mahimahi she'd prepared. "Those kids seemed to be having fun today."

Mary-Kate smiled up at the older woman, glad that someone liked her idea. "They sure did. And they'll continue to do so!" She threw a challenging look at Dane.

"So tell me all you did today," he invited, a cynical look in his eyes.

Mary-Kate refused to be daunted by his look. She launched into the time they'd spent at the beach, the knowledge she'd shared about shells with the children, some of the facts the older ones had shared with her. Then she spoke about the craft projects she was planning, the games they played.

Dane spoke little during dinner, his eyes watching Mary-Kate as she explained each detail of her plans, and regaled him with each minute of her day. From time to time genuine amusement touched his eyes, but generally he watched her through skeptical eyes.

"And so after that I thought we'd look for wildflowers and categorize them," she finished. Despite his daunting look, her enthusiasm spilled out.

"Where are you planning to find these flowers?"

"Wherever they grow—by the beach, most likely; you seem to have the rest of the island cultivated. But I need to look at one of your books on flora before then."

"Be my guest."

When dinner was finished, Mary-Kate hurried to the study to select the books she wanted. Dane had several good ones on plants and flowers, and she was sure she could study enough to recognize any she might see on their upcoming nature hike.

Dane joined her in the study, but after only a few moments Mary-Kate looked up. His eyes bore down on her; he ignored the work at his desk. She flushed, conscious of his comment earlier about her disturbing him. Not wanting to give rise to such a comment again, she rose, books in hand.

"I'll just read in the other room. I can concentrate better if someone isn't staring at me all the time."

He smiled mockingly, but said nothing.

Mary-Kate sat on the floor before the couch, spreading the books around her, opened to pages of the plants indigenous to the Hawaiian Islands, looking for any she'd seen since arriving on Manahakaloi. She took notes, studied drawings and pictures, and memorized facts about each of the different flowers.

Maybe tomorrow, before dinner, she'd walk around a little, and see if she could locate any of the flowers, so that she'd know where to take the children.

"You going to sit here all night?" Dane's hard voice sounded from the doorway.

Mary-Kate blinked and looked up at him. Slowly her mind left the plant world and focused in on him.

"Is it late?"

"After eleven."

She rubbed her hands across her face; her eyes were dry and gritty.

"I was getting tired, but didn't realize it was so late." She tried to rise, but her foot gave way under her, asleep.

"Ouch!" she exclaimed as she sat down hard. "My foot's gone to sleep. Blast it!"

Dane moved in and reached down to pull her up, holding her steady as the foot in question began its agonizing awakening process.

"How long is this little act going to go on?" he said softly in her ear.

She jerked back, stumbling and sitting hard on the arm of the couch. "What little act? My foot did fall asleep!" It was tingling now, alive with a thousand hot needles, all pricking her. She shook it to hasten the process.

"I meant the dedicated teacher bit. You want to run a one-room schoolhouse this autumn?"

"No, I don't! I'm leaving, remember? This summer camp idea is just temporary, to help out."

"Help out who?"

"The mothers who want some extra money, and me."

"I'll pay for your passage to Oahu." He stood too near, threateningly near.

"I'll pay my own way, thank you anyway. Now I'm tired, and I'm going to bed."

She stood, and almost sat back down. Dane towered over her, not a foot away, and he wasn't moving. Mary-Kate faced him defiantly, reluctant to push her way by him, afraid of what would happen if she touched him, if he touched her.

He did not make it difficult for her, however; he stepped aside, his eyes never leaving her.

"Good night," she mumbled as she walked with dignity to her room, wishing he'd kissed her again, and annoyed with herself for feeling that way.

CHAPTER NINE

BREAKFAST was a strain the next morning. Dane had stacks of papers before him, and barely glanced at Mary-Kate when she entered. She ate her rolls quietly, not wanting to start the day off on the wrong foot. She had plenty to think about with the summer camp; she wouldn't worry about his attitude just yet.

"When are you going?" Dane asked as she gazed out of the window, lost in thought of plans for arts and crafts.

"Going?" She blinked at him, struck again by his strong good looks, even when his eyes were bleak and his emotions held in tight check as they were now.

"To the compound. I'm driving down in a few minutes; if you're ready, you can go with me."

"Thanks. I thought I'd have to walk again." She smiled at him, but he did not return the gesture. Only turned back to his papers, gathering them into a large stack.

As they drove the short distance to the compound, Mary-Kate couldn't help but think of what might have been. If she stayed, they could drive together each day, he to his job, she to hers. At night they could discuss what they'd done during the day. Sometimes it might be fun to walk the way, and so have longer to talk, to discuss things while enjoying the pleasures of the warm evenings on the island.

Dane didn't speak when they reached the compound, and Mary-Kate only bade him a quiet, "Bye for now," before heading for the tables already set up for the summer camp.

The day flew by.

"It looks like it's due to storm bad, tonight or tomorrow," Joyce said as she picked up little Joy in the afternoon. "If so, don't try to come down tomorrow. We'll keep the kids inside. Next day should be okay."

"If it rains, I'll stay home." Mary-Kate knew there was no place for the group of children if they couldn't have their meetings outside. They used a couple of makeshift tables and benches from the barbecue for worktables, but it had become increasingly difficult during the afternoon to keep things on them. The breeze from the west was steadily rising. Puffs of wind had blown off the drawings, scattered the light shells they'd cleaned, and whipped hair before eyes trying to see to color.

Mary-Kate glanced around the area one last time, looking for anything that had sailed away. All things had been secured for the night. She waved at the last of her little friends, and started off for the big white house. She didn't see the jeep, and wouldn't wait around in the hope that Dane would come for her.

It was early yet; dinner wouldn't be for a couple
of hours. Maybe she'd scout around a little and
see if she could find the wildflowers she wanted
to locate for their nature trip. If it rained tomorrow, she'd take the children on the outing
the following day.

It was pleasant to walk in the strong breeze.
The intense heat normally found, even this late
in the afternoon, was missing. The air was actually cooler. Large gray clouds that had been
building in the west all day now obliterated the
sun. The sky was gray from one side to the other,
but a light silvery gray. It didn't look as if rain
was imminent.

Mary-Kate took one of the roads from the
compound that she'd not traveled before. She
would walk along for a while then double back.
Perhaps it would connect with another road that
would lead her back to Dane's house. The island
seemed to have many dirt roads crisscrossing it.
They'd been built to carry the trucks into the
pineapple fields for easy access to the fruit.

Just as she'd suspected, the road joined up with
another dirt road. She turned right, toward the
house. The road veered right, then turned left.
Still she trudged along; it would probably veer
again. Another road. Should she take this road
or keep on the one she was on already?

Endless rows of pineapple stretched out in all
directions. The rows in the field to the left were
parallel to the road, in the field to the right they

were perpendicular. Was there a reason for the alternating planting? She'd have to ask Dane.

Ahead in the distance was sugarcane. Mary-Kate knew she was going in the right direction. Hadn't she walked through the cane before first seeing his house?

The wind was rising. The dust from the dirt roads swirled around her feet, now and then rising in a whirlwind, blinding her for a few seconds, until the funnel danced away. Her skirt whipped around her legs, sometimes plastered against them, other times billowing out in the air.

There were no wildflowers along this way. Time to get back home. The wind was growing stronger. Mary-Kate looked at the sugarcane. There was no way through. The tall, leafy green cane formed an impenetrable wall before her. She turned and followed the road that ran alongside. Surely there'd be a way through soon?

The sound of the wind rustling in the cane was loud. For a moment a *frisson* of fear touched her. Surely she knew the way back to the house? Was she going to have to retrace her steps all the way back to the compound first?

She turned around, confused. Rows upon rows of pineapple stretched out before her. How many turnings had she made? How many roads had she crossed, how many had she turned on? Where was she? Nothing looked familiar. Nothing gave her a clue as to where she was or how to find Dane's house.

She had not seen another soul during her walk.
Was that odd? Weren't the men harvesting the
pineapple? Shouldn't there be men in some of
the fields? Or was the island so large that they
were all working out of sight from where she
stood?

Though, with the high wind, maybe they'd all
taken off to go surfing. Where was the beach?
Mary-Kate turned back and started walking
again, the tall sugarcane on her right, the open
pineapple fields to her left. She walked briskly,
now facing the wind.

Sand and grit flew up and stung her face. She
kept her eyes narrowed against the debris,
searching around to find another person, to see
something she recognized that would show her
the way back to Dane's house. She walked for
hours, growing tired fighting against the constant wind; now it was at her back, now at one
side.

The rustle in the sugarcane was monotonous,
loud and hypnotic. Mary-Kate knew she was lost,
but did not know how to find her way out.
Sooner or later, she'd reach the sea and could
follow the coast around until she found either
the cove beneath the house or the inlet where the
ships docked.

At least she wouldn't starve; there was fruit
aplenty for the taking. She wouldn't freeze; even
though the air temperature was the coolest she'd
felt since arriving in Hawaii, it was scarcely cold.
If she was stuck out all night, it looked as if she'd

get very wet. The storm the other afternoon had been brief, quickly passing. It could be a lot worse.

What a fool she'd been to go exploring alone, without telling anyone! She should have asked Nora or Joyce or even Dane where to look for flowers, how to find her way back. She only knew one route from the house to the compound, but, according to the children, there were several, so she'd thought she'd be all right.

She stepped into the edge of the pineapple plot, and broke one of the fruits from its plant. The outside was hard, the skin rough, but she didn't care. She was getting hungry, and surely Dane wouldn't begrudge her one pineapple?

But how would she peel it?

Damn, if it wasn't one thing it was another! She started up again, carrying her fruit, looking for a rock or sharp stick that she could use to skin the pineapple. Ahead of her in the distance beyond the sugarcane she saw a roof. She paused. Had she come full circle? Was that the processing plant? The roof was large, high. She frowned; she didn't remember any sugarcane near the processing plant. Slowly she proceeded.

Stepping free of the cane, Mary-Kate was almost knocked over as the wind whipped past her with a fury. She caught her breath, bent over to combat the strong surge of air. Then her eyes narrowed as she took in what was before her.

A tarmac runway. The wind sock blowing straight out, swinging wildly as the wind veered from one direction to the other. The high corrugated metal building was a hangar, she guessed. Hurrying along, she found a door in the side. It was unlocked.

The serenity of the interior was shattering after the fury of the wind. It was calm, peaceful and quiet inside the large building, though the wailing of the wind set an eerie background. Before her in the gloom stood the blue and white plane she'd seen the other morning. The other two mornings.

Mary-Kate closed the door behind her, blinking in the near darkness. Her hand found a light switch, and she flicked it on. Nothing. She opened the door, and searched the interior with the twilight streaming in. There was a workbench against the wall, and on it a lantern.

She left the door open, and walked over to the workbench. A two-minute search located matches and, crossing her fingers that the lantern was filled, she lifted the glass and struck the match. The mantle caught, and bright light filled the dim interior. She settled the glass in place, and took the lantern, turning to survey the hangar.

It was a big building, but not huge. The plane took up most of the floor space, but there were workbenches, lockers and boxes around three walls. The fourth one was the main hangar door. It looked as if it rolled up, following tracks that crossed the ceiling.

Mary-Kate closed the side door, shutting out the wind and the fury of the impending storm, and turned to examine the plane. It had to be the same one she'd seen. What was it doing here? She sat down. She knew what it was doing here. It was parked here. This was its hangar. It belonged here, belonged to the island owner. Dane Carmichael had had the means to take her off the island from day one. Someone had even flown off a couple of days ago.

She frowned. It was the day he'd not come in for supper, the day she'd been so excited to explain her plan. He'd flown it. He'd lied to her. But why? Her heart lurched, then settled in a slow beat. The ache was slight, but persistent. She felt hurt and disappointed that he'd lied to her. There had been no need.

Mary-Kate sat for a long time, staring at the plane, as if it could give her answers. Why had Dane not told her about the plane? Why had he insisted there was no way off the island except by the supply boat? She rubbed her forehead, confusion rampant.

She sighed; no answers were forthcoming, only more questions. She got up from the hard concrete floor, and walked around the building, examining it in detail. She found a set of utensils. At least she could eat her pineapple. There was running water, so she could drink. Most of the items in the building were there to service the airplane, but a couple of lockers held clothes. She finished her tour at the door she'd used to enter. Opening it a crack, she saw it had grown darker outside. The wind was still blowing hard, and the sky was a boiling mass of dark clouds. Even as she watched, the storm came. Torrents of lashing, driving rain pounded across the landscape, across the tarmac, in a line as sharply defined as a drawing. It headed for the hangar.

Mary-Kate slammed the door shut seconds before she heard the pounding on the roof, on the corrugated sides, the small windows set high on the wall. She shivered, glad after all that she was not out in the rain. It would have been a miserable night.

She ate the pineapple, washing the sticky juice from her face and hands, using the nearby sink. Moving the lantern to the center of the cleared space, she set it carefully on the floor, then studied the plane.

She stepped up on the wing and tried the door. It opened easily to her touch, and she stepped inside. It smelt of leather, and fuel oil and wood. She moved to one of the seats, and sat down. It felt good. She found the release lever, and re-clined the back. For a makeshift shelter, this couldn't be beaten.

She closed her eyes, listening to the drum of the rain on the metal roof of the hangar. It was steady, furious, pounding. Thankful she was not out in it, she hoped no one else was.

Mary-Kate shivered a little. She didn't think it got cold in Hawaii, but the storm was cooling the air. She lay back in the seat, dreaming of sunny days, of wide white beaches, and of what she and the children could do for the next couple of weeks.

And of leaving on the supply boat.

She would hate to leave. She had grown to love the island, the few people she'd met, the slow pace of life. And Dane Carmichael. She hugged her secret to herself. She didn't know when it had happened, or why, but she loved him—everything about him, from his bad temper, to his determination to think badly of her, to his sexy body. She had never loved anyone with quite the passion and longing she did this man.

And for nothing. He didn't even want her to stay. He didn't love her. Real life wasn't like fairy tales. Dane loved Melissa, who didn't love him. And she, Mary-Kate, loved him. She sighed, tears threatening. She would miss him so much when she left. But she would never forget him. She would remember him all her life.

She cocked her head, listening. Was that a dog's bark? Suddenly the door in the side of the hangar flew open, and banged against the inside wall. She sat up, startled. Had the wind caught it? Hadn't she latched it properly? She stepped to the door of the plane, and peered out. Marco barked gleefully, running to the plane, tail wagging.

Dane filled the doorway, water streaming from him, while behind him the lashing fury of the storm raged. His eyes darted frantically everywhere, then followed the dog.

"Mary-Kate?" he roared.

"What?" she replied, delight swelling in her breasts to see him. She was safe now.

His eyes moved to her, then narrowed as he took in the scene. He moved inside and slammed the door shut. The storm's ferocity was muted by the building. In silence Mary-Kate watched the man who had lied to her. Desperately wanting him to explain away the lies, she moved down the plane's wing to the concrete floor. Marco bumped into her, and she patted his wet head.

"What the hell are you doing here?" Dane asked, deadly quiet, dripping water where he stood. His face was black with anger, his eyes steely shafts piercing the gloom.

"Seeking shelter from the storm. How did you find me?"

"I've been searching the whole damn island for you! When I saw the light in the hangar, I thought I'd check it out. Marco raised a fuss when we drew nearer. There are four others out searching for you, too."

"Oh." She leaned against the plane. She hadn't thought anyone would miss her. "I'm safe," she said lamely.

"Not if I get my hands on you!" he muttered, and turned to go back out.

"Dane, wait! Don't leave me!"

"I'm not going anywhere; I'm going to try to reach the others on the jeep radio. No sense in risking lives further now that I know you're safe. This storm is a killer."

Mary-Kate leaned guiltily against the side of the plane, watching the outside door for his return. She hadn't wanted anyone put in danger because of her. She was safe—she hadn't thought they would mount a search. For all Dane knew she could have stayed at Joyce's or Lisa's for the night.

Dane returned, slamming the door behind him. He was dripping water, and shook his head to clear his sight. Mary-Kate watched silently as he headed to one of the lockers and snatched it open.

"Dane, why didn't you tell me about the plane?" Mary-Kate asked, determined to bring the matter out into the open.

"I had my reasons."

"I've been stuck on this island for days, when all along I could have got back to the yacht. Someone even flew this thing somewhere the other day; I could have had a ride out to the other islands."

"Not now, Mary-Kate." His voice sounded tired.

"Yes, right now. I want to know why you lied to me!"

"I'm tired, wet, hungry, and not in the mood to listen to your histrionics. I'll discuss it with you later," he bit out between clenched teeth. "I also want to know why you took off to go sightseeing when a huge storm was brewing. Without telling anyone. I had people looking all over for you—risking their necks to try to save yours!"

"I didn't know it was going to storm. I was looking for the wildflowers. If I'd been allowed to leave when I first wanted to, I wouldn't have been here to get lost and have all your people risking their necks!'' Mary-Kate yelled back, guilt making her defensive.

Dane sighed, and unbuttoned his shirt; shrugging out of it, he balled it up and threw it angrily toward the wall. She watched him out of angry eyes, furious that he hadn't answered her—and not a little guilty because of getting lost. She should have gone straight home.

His eyes fixed on hers as he unfastened the wet shorts. She held his gaze, conscious of his wide shoulders, the damp muscles of his chest. When the pants parted, she gave a small gasp and turned her back on him, holding on to her sanity with every ounce in her.

She wanted to throw herself against him, to dry his skin, and feel it beneath her fingers, beneath her lips. She longed for his hard, steely eyes to soften into silver smoke so that she knew he wanted her. As she wanted him...to feel his hands on her body, bringing her to rapture and ecstasy. She longed for one night in his arms. But she would not let him know that.

Her mind a careful blank, she refused to let her desire build any more. She wanted him to explain why he had never told her about the plane, why he hadn't offered at least to contact someone for her when he had flown the plane out the other day. Maybe there would be a good explanation. *Maybe.*

She shivered again; it was decidedly cooler. She wrapped her arms around her, wishing she had a sweater or light jacket.

"Cold?" His hand grasped her upper arm, pulling her slowly around to face him. He was dressed in dry shorts and a brightly colored Hawaiian shirt. She glanced down. They didn't look like his, somehow.

"These belong to Roy. Are you cold?" he answered her inquiring look, and repeated his question.

Mary-Kate jerked her arm free and stepped back, into the side of the plane. "No, I'm fine. I still want an answer; why didn't you tell me about the plane? If it has a radio, couldn't I have contacted the outside world? Dammit, Dane, you should have told me, you should have told me before——"

She looked away, appalled at what she'd almost said: You should have told me before I fell in love with you. Before it was too late.

"Before what?" His voice was hard as his hands caught her shoulders and swung her around before him. "Before *what*?"

"N-n-nothing," she murmured, refusing to meet his gaze, her eyes on the strong column of his neck. His hands were hard on her shoulders, holding her, capturing her.

"You forced your way on to my island, refusing to leave with your friends. I was furious when you came to the door. I'd had it with pretty women trying to snare me into marriage just so they could help me spend my money. I decided I'd do nothing to help you. Let you see what it would be like if you did get your way. Dammit, Mary-Kate, I didn't want you on my island!''

Her face moved up at that, frustration building.

"I did not force my way on to your damn island! I was left, abandoned, deserted! As much as you hate it, I had no choice in the matter. What was I supposed to do, camp out on the beach until you and your dogs came to chase me away? I didn't have a boat to escape with. I thought you finally believed me. I'm not the one who's been lying—it's you. You told me there was no way off the island, nor any way to contact anyone. You lied to me, Dane Carmichael, and there was no need!''

Mary-Kate felt perilously close to tears; she dragged her eyes away from his, looking down at her feet, at the dog sitting patiently beside his master, eyes following the two of them. She was conscious of Dane's hands on her shoulders.

He watched her for several long moments, then, when she refused to meet his gaze, his hands moved down her arms. "You're cold; get in the plane. There are some blankets there. Marco, stay!''

The left side of the plane dipped as he stepped on the wing, pulling her along behind him. He seemed to fill the small body of the little plane when he stepped inside. He pushed her into one of the seats, and went to the back. Returning with two blankets, he sank heavily into the seat across the narrow aisle. Tossing her one of the blankets, he leaned back, head resting on the seat back.

Tension rose in the small confines of the plane. Mary-Kate glanced nervously at him as she spread the blanket over her, wanting him to say something, anything. But he remained silent.

"Why didn't you tell me about the plane?" she finally asked gently.

Dane moved his head, and opened his eyes to see her. "At first I was mad that you had stayed behind. I wasn't going to make it easy for you to leave."

When he said nothing more, Mary-Kate prodded, "I told you I hadn't stayed behind, I had been left. You must believe that by now?"

"By the time I did believe it, I didn't want you to go any earlier than you had to." His voice was low. His eyes were mere slits, studying her across the narrow aisle, studying her reactions.

"That doesn't make sense. You can't wait for me to be gone."

"I'll miss you when you go," he admitted softly.

Her heart lurched as she stared at him in the dim light; had she heard correctly? "What?"

"Given other circumstances, other times, we might have been good together," he said. "I will miss you when you go."

"What circumstances?" she asked suspiciously, her heart pounding at the soft, tender note in his voice. Her hopes flared. Maybe he wasn't indifferent to her; maybe there was hope for them.

"If you were rich. If you had traveled the world and found it lacking. If you owned half the island and I the other half."

"You're a cynic, Dane Carmichael. You've been unfortunate in the women you've known, but all are not like them. Look at Lisa, at Joyce, at Nora. They all live here, and happily. Why do you think other women can't?"

"Money does funny things to people. They suddenly want to spend it."

"I don't think much of your taste in women!" Mary-Kate retorted waspishly. She wasn't flattered to be classified with those other teachers who had tried to capture the boss—or with Melissa.

He smiled, his eyes lightening in amusement. "I guess I don't either. But you're something, honey. Maybe not in the same category?"

"Definitely not!" Mary-Kate longed to have him hold her again, longed to tell him she loved him, that she wanted to stay more than anything. But that would put her in with all the others, and she had too much pride for that. She'd leave as he'd asked her to, head held high, pride intact.

And heartbroken.

The pounding of the rain on the roof sounded louder, the slam of water against the side of the building reverberated sharply. Mary-Kate shivered, eyeing the building. "It's an awful storm, isn't it? Will the building stand?"

"Yes to both. I had the devil's own time getting here; the jeep wanted to wander off the road. The rain's coming down in sheets, and most of the roads are now muddy strips along the cultivated area."

"When I knew I was lost, I thought I would be caught out in it. But I wasn't worried; I thought it would be just a mild tropical storm, like the one we had the other afternoon."

If she hadn't found this shelter, there was no telling what she would have found out in the storm.

"It's part of a typhoon—pretty far south, and not the right time of year, but there it is. I'm glad you weren't caught in it; it's dangerous. That's why we were looking for you."

"How did you know I was out there?"

"When you didn't show up for dinner, I went to the compound. I talked to several women there, including Joyce, who told me when you left. I got Mike and Roy and two others who have jeeps to start crisscrossing the island, looking for you."

"You reached them, by the jeep radio?"

"Yes, they're all safely home by now."

Mary-Kate glanced over to him, startled to find his eyes still on her. "I didn't mean to put so many people out."

"And what did you mean to do? What have you meant to do all along?"

She drew a shaky breath, and shook her head. "All I wanted was a Hawaiian summer. It seemed so easy last spring. I didn't want to meet you, get stuck here.''

"I know that full well. You'll be going soon; you needn't make it so clear." His voice was hard again.

He'd misinterpreted her words, but she didn't correct him. No point in it. Better if he thought she didn't want to stay rather than that her heart was breaking at the thought of leaving. Wouldn't he scoff at that?

She lay against the seat, savoring every second with him, saving up memories for the long nights ahead. She could hear his breathing in the quiet confines of the little plane, over the drum of the rain. She could smell the special scent of him: pineapple, sunshine and salt air.

She'd thought of him as a pirate when she'd first seen him, and he'd proved to be more like one than she'd first thought. He lived like one, doing everything to suit himself, without a care for others and their feelings. No, that was not true. He did care, but he'd been hurt in the past, and would not let that happen again. He had not known her feelings would become involved.

And he'd never know it, she vowed. Better to have him think her a gold digger who had failed than to realize the old-fashioned girl from Iowa had fallen in love with him.

"So you know all about the plane now. No words of recrimination?" She shook her head, afraid to speak for fear that the tears trembling in her eyes would fall. "No declaration of for-

giveness and undying love?'' his voice mocked—
herself? Himself?

She chanced her voice.

"Love is very special, Dane. Not to be scoffed
at. It doesn't come to everyone, and it is not returned every time. But if it ever comes to you,
you must learn to trust it, and put aside your
fears of a repetition of the past. Love is trust,
and trust is a part of love.''

"And have you ever loved?'' he asked in the
darkness.

"Only once, and it wasn't returned,'' she
whispered after a long moment.

"More fool he.''

CHAPTER TEN

THE lantern gave off its steady glow from the floor of the hangar. Inside the plane, it was much darker. They could hear the frenzy of the storm as it played against the tin roof, along the corrugated metal walls. The confines of the small plane muffled the sounds, giving a feeling of increased safety against nature's elements.

"Mary-Kate, when the storm's over, I'll take you to the Big Island, if you like. Fly you there right away." Dane's voice was quiet, without inflection.

Mary-Kate tried to see him in the dim light, but could only see his outline; she couldn't see his face, see what expression he wore. Was it a trick of some sort? Or was he finally letting her leave? Depression washed through her at the thought. She didn't want to leave. She'd been saying she did, but she didn't.

When she didn't answer, he reached out for her, lifting her from her seat, and settling back in his with her in his lap, her legs over the arm of his chair, her head cradled against his shoulder.

"Or, if you would care to stay a little longer, you can still go on the supply ship. It would be a shame to disappoint the children, don't you think?"

162

His hand drew trails of fire down her arm, as he moved it slowly up and down her soft skin.

"Only for the children?" she said, so softly that he had to bend his head to hear her.

"No. We never did get our walk along the beach after dark." He kissed her forehead.

Mary-Kate closed her eyes, scarcely able to breathe. Slowly her hand crept up to his shoulder.

"We could go skinny-dipping in the cove, just you and me." He kissed her cheeks, her eyelids.

Mary-Kate felt her insides begin to melt, her breathing to cease. Her heart tripped double time, the blood rushing in her ears. She could scarcely contain her delight. Dane was making love to her. After all she'd yelled at him, he was still interested in her.

She should stop now, but didn't want to. She should pull back and agree to the plane ride out first thing. But the thought of a few more days with Dane was too tempting. She wanted to stay. Let herself have two more weeks.

"Maybe you could teach me the hula?" she said as her hand threaded itself in his thick hair and she pulled his head down to find her waiting lips.

The drumming of the rain was drowned by the drumming of her blood as it pounded in her ears. His mouth was hot and sweet and demanding. His lips moved against hers, provoking a response Mary-Kate was helpless to deny. She rubbed against him in her pleasure, delighting in the touch of his hair in her hands, reveling in the feel of his lips against hers, his arm holding her safely, the strong legs supporting her.

When his hand dropped from her arm to her stomach, she gave a soft gasp, muffled against the hot moisture of his mouth. He took advantage of her gasp to invade the sweet warmth within as his tongue sought hers, caressed it, teased it.

Mary-Kate moved against him again, naturally, as if seeking more than the devastation of his kiss. Dane's hand rose to cup her breast, his thumb rasping against the soft cotton covering, erecting her nipple, feeding the flame that glowed deep within her. His hand couldn't feel enough as he fondled and stroked the swelling mound.

Releasing her mouth, his lips trailed passionate kisses down her neck to the top of her dress. Pushing aside the material, he sought and found the erect peak awaiting his touch. Taking it in his mouth, he pressed against her, sucking gently, his teeth scraping tenderly, tantalizingly over her rosy nub. Mary-Kate felt the pull deep within her, and held his head against her to enjoy the delicious feeling as long as she could.

She was hot and constricted in the clothes she wore. Gone was the chill from the storm. She wanted to be free, and to feel Dane's heated skin against her own. Slowly one hand moved from his head to his shirt, unfastening the buttons, spreading the material away from his chest.

It was as if they were one in thought. When his chest was bared, he drew back and pulled her against him, her bare breasts against his hard chest muscles. Mary-Kate moved against him, as a kitten would rub against her. Enchanted with the way he felt, she wanted more. Hungrily she sought his mouth, seeking the pleasure his touch evoked.

"God, you're beautiful!" His voice was muffled against her mouth as she found his.

Stop, the voice of sanity sounded, before it is too late. But it is already too late, much too late... The refrain repeated itself in her head, and she gave herself up to the ecstasy Dane's touch promised.

Dane's fingers threaded themselves in her curls, bringing her mouth to his in a kiss almost punishing in its intensity. Mary-Kate had never known such emotions; she was overwhelmed and wild, moving only to his guidance, only to his touch.

He broke their kiss, holding her head back away from him as he looked down into her half-closed eyes, drugged with passion. She frowned slightly; why had he stopped? Moving ineffectively, she tried to reach him again.

"Mary-Kate. Look at me." His voice was soft, urgent. She opened her eyes, and tried to see him in the gloom. "I want you. I want you right now."

She nodded slowly as she moved back toward him, longing for another kiss, for his hands to make their magic on her skin again, for whatever he wanted from her.

"No strings, no promises." His voice was hard, cold.

Mary-Kate watched him, wanting him as she had never wanted anything in her life. "No strings, no promises," she whispered in return.

He stood them on their feet, and reached for the bottom of the seat. Releasing a lever, he tilted the entire seat forward, opening a large flat section of flooring. Spreading the blankets on the carpeting, he tugged her gently down.

Mary-Kate went into his arms as if she'd been doing it her whole life. She felt alive and loved within his embrace. Eagerly she reached up for his kiss, sighing with hot pleasure when his hand covered her breast. She could go on like this forever. Never coming back to reality. It was an enchanted time, belonging only to her and Dane.

When he discarded his shirt, she took pleasure in the feel of his strong muscles across his back, his skin heated from the passion they shared. She arched her back to help him push her dress below her waist, moving in a mindless rhythm against his mouth as he learned her body, kissing first one breast, then the other, his tongue caressing every inch of her skin. From her peaks to the valley between, down to the circle of her navel. His breath was hot against her skin, heating it to fever pitch. She drew in huge gulps of air, trying to cool her heated body, to regain some measure of sanity in the wild ecstasy his touch wrought.

The whoop of the siren was shattering in the enclosed hangar. Its wail rose and fell as it screamed its warning. Mary-Kate started in fright, screaming out, her hands covering her ears as the penetrating sound filled the plane, filled the hangar.

"Hell!" Dane was up in a flash, grabbing his shirt. He raced out of the plane and to the side door. It didn't close behind him.

Mary-Kate was stunned with the suddenness of it all. She pulled up her dress and, hands over her ears, moved to the doorway of the little plane. She could see the rain blowing in the side door, a wide spot of wet concrete already testifying to the intensity of the storm. Marco was in the door, barking, scarcely heard over the wail of the siren.

Where was the siren's noise coming from? Why was it sounding? God, it was deafening! She climbed down from the plane, ran swiftly to the door, and peered out. Where was Dane? She could see nothing, and the wind blew the rain in so hard that she was already wet. She could hear the siren on the outside, too. It must cover half the island. Was it an alarm? What was it for?

"Dane?" she called, trying to see something in the stormy darkness. There was nothing. "Dane!"

Twin lights from the jeep careened around the corner. He drew to an abrupt stop beside her, and opened the door. "There's an emergency, at the harbor. You want to come with me or stay here?"

"I'm coming." She didn't want to stay with that siren blaring, all alone.

"Extinguish the lantern, and hurry. I've got to get there!"

She ran to the lantern and turned it off. Waiting only a moment to make sure it was extinguished, she ran back to the door. Slamming it shut behind her, she checked to make sure it was latched. Dane had her door open for her, and Marco was already in the car. Mary-Kate was soaked by the time she took her seat.

"It's awful out!" she exclaimed, fastening her seat belt snugly. Reaching up to wring out her hair, she stared in disbelief through the windshield. The rain was like a waterfall—strong, solid, cold.

The siren continued its mournful wail, diminished only somewhat by the storm's fury around the jeep. The rain fell more heavily than Mary-Kate had ever seen it; how Dane could see through the windshield was beyond her.

The wind buffeted the jeep as it slithered and slid along the muddy roads. How did he know where he was going? It was black as pitch. She could not distinguish anything. The feeble headlights were swallowed up by the darkness. Was he driving blind?

"What happened?" she asked, gripping her hands tightly as they slid four feet to the left.

"Ship's aground at the harbor. Misjudged the distance and ran aground on the point. Taking on water. Mike sounded the warning. When I called in he said he's already notified the coast guard, but it'll be hours before any cutter can get here. We're going to see if the crew needs help.''

''What do you mean?''

''We'll take the launch. If there are injuries, or if the ship is in danger of sinking, we can bring them to the island.''

''Dane, that's suicidal in this weather!''

He grinned in the faint light of the dashboard. ''Not really. Dangerous, yes, but we won't take any unnecessary chances. Can't have people dying on your doorstep.''

Mary-Kate was silent for a few minutes, marveling at his driving skill. It was too dark to see anything. The rain seemed to soak up the lights from the jeep, and everything looked the same to her—black and blurry. ''How can you find your way?'' She would have been lost as soon as they'd lost sight of the hangar.

''I know the island; we're almost there. I don't want to have to worry about you while I'm worrying about the ship. You go to Joyce's or Lisa's.''

Mary-Kate glanced over at him. ''Can't I help somehow? Make coffee or something?''

''They'll be doing that at one of the women's houses; do it there.''

''Okay.'' She relapsed into silence, watching the wipers try to clear the water from the windshield, still hearing the siren. ''I can still hear that siren,'' she said.

''There are several alarm signals in various places across the island. You can hear them no

matter where you are. It's our warning system.
Everyone finds out what the emergency is, and
then rallies around to help. We did it this way in
case something happens during the day when
everyone is at work, scattered across the island.''

"You won't do anything foolish and...and
heroic, will you?'' Mary-Kate couldn't help
asking. Fear for the recklessness of the man made
her.

He chuckled, and shook his head. "Nope.
Only do what's needed.''

Mary-Kate was not content with that answer,
but she let the matter drop. He'd do what he
wanted in any event. No sense in letting him know
how worried she was about him.

When they reached the compound, it was sur-
realistic. Bright mercury-vapor lamps at the
corners of the processing plant illuminated the
yard. The wail of the sirens screamed over the
sound of the storm. Men and women were
moving about in the rain, the plant itself was lit
up as if in full operation. Beyond, Mary-Kate
could see lights dancing near the wharf.

"They've opened up the plant; go there.'' Dane
grabbed her and gave her a hard kiss, then left.
She saw him plunge into the middle of the group
of men in the yard.

Sitting would get nothing done, so she opened
the door, and was almost blown away by the
fierce wind. She fastened the door, and turned
to the building. The water was running down her
neck and back by the time she reached the plant.

She ran inside, shaking her head to clear it of water. Mercifully the sirens went dead.

The scene before her reminded her of Red Cross drills. Tables had been set up, benches and cots along the far wall. The machinery and conveyor belts were silent and still. Women were stacking blankets and bandages on one table, others were preparing coffee and sandwiches. Mary-Kate saw Joyce, and hurried over.

"Can I help?"

"Sure; grab a knife, and start on these sandwiches."

"Have you heard anything?" Mary-Kate asked as she began.

"Japanese ship missed the warning light, somehow, and ran aground. Or maybe the wind is so strong it just blew it ashore. In any event, the ship is taking water. That's all I heard."

"Are they in danger of sinking?"

"Don't know yet. That's what they're going out to check for."

Mary-Kate nodded, and set to work making sandwiches. She worried about Dane and what he and his men would be up to. Trying to ignore the adventure stories she'd read all her life, where men risked their lives to save others, she prayed, Please, God, let everyone get out safely.

When they'd used up the supplies, they covered the sandwiches to keep them fresh. Then the women sat quietly on the benches, talking desultorily as they waited. Suddenly there was an explosion from the sea.

"Oh, no!" One of the women jumped up and ran to the door, two or three others closely behind her. In seconds they returned, drenched.

"Looks like something blew on the boat; there's a fire there now."

Mary-Kate rubbed her hands against her dress, trying to still her shakes. She was scared for Dane. Was he all right? She glanced around. Each of these women had a man she loved out there; each was worried, concerned. But each of those men knew they had someone waiting for them; they would not take silly risks. But Dane was alone. And he was their leader. He would take risks if he thought it appropriate.

Please, God, let him get through safely.

The night was long. Before dawn the first of the Japanese sailors reached the processing plant. Some were merely shaken. Others were injured from the explosion or the fire. Another load arrived.

Mary-Kate helped with first aid, soothing on burn lotion, lightly covering the burns, cleaning cuts and bandaging them. Each time a new group arrived, she searched for Dane. Once she saw Mike.

"How's Dane?" she called.

He gave a thumbs-up sign, his eyes searching for Lisa.

"She's over there, by the coffee," Mary-Kate told him, turning back to the young man she was treating for shock.

And so the night ended and dawn arrived. But a stormy dawn: dark and wet and slow to show. Gradually the darkness lifted, showing a dreary grey morning. The rain continued pouring, the wind gusted and swirled.

Then she saw him. He looked dog tired, his shirt torn, soaked, his hair matted against his forehead, his shoulders sagging. Dane helped in another of the Japanese crew, and waited until he was lying down before moving.

Mary-Kate grabbed a cup of coffee for him and hurried over. His eyes were dull with fatigue, and he merely nodded and reached for the cup. She watched him anxiously, longing to touch him, to comfort him, to ask him to rest a moment. But she had no right to do so. And she didn't need a set down here, before all the other people.

"Are you almost finished?" she asked.

"We can only take a few off at a time. The launch is small. The skipper of the ship won't leave. I think it's safe now, but it burned a bit. The tide's going out, so he should be stuck good and tight until later. Mike's taking the launch now. I needed a rest—almost crashed it on the last go round."

"Dane, help!" Joyce ran into the doorway, frantically looking for Dane.

He hurried over, Mary-Kate at his heels. "What is it?"

"Lisa—she went back for some more coffee, and fell. I think she's hurt bad. Come see."

Dane and Mary-Kate followed Joyce across the compound. Palm fronds broke from the tall trees and crashed to the ground, then were whipped across the surface by the strong wind. Mary-Kate dodged two as she hurried after them.

Lisa was lying on the stairs to her house, her face streaked with rain and mud. She was clutching her swollen abdomen.

"Easy, Lisa; what happened, where do you hurt?" Dane knelt beside her, Mary-Kate and Joyce on the other side.

"I hit the baby when I fell. What if I killed my baby?" She was almost hysterical with worry.

"You're probably all right, and your baby, too," Mary-Kate said practically. "Babies float in a sac designed for just such accidents." She reached down and took Lisa's hand. "Don't worry, your baby will be fine."

"I think I'm having contractions," Lisa mumbled, gripping Mary-Kate's hand. "Could I have started them by the fall?"

"Possibly; just relax." Mary-Kate's voice was calm, but the look she cast Dane was not. She didn't know much about babies, only what she'd picked up from her sisters when they had had theirs. It could be dangerous for Lisa to have her baby two months early, and in such a storm.

"I'll take her to the plant; we'll watch her, and have the coast guard airlift her out with the others," Dane decided.

Mary-Kate hurried ahead to prepare a cot for Lisa, while Dane carried her to the processing plant. Mary-Kate and Joyce made her comfortable.

"You'll be okay, Lisa, just hang in there," she said softly, hoping it would be true.

Hours passed, and the activity continued. Fewer and fewer injured were brought in. Dane left again, but Mike didn't appear. Then the first of the helicopters sounded, landing in the compound. Dane motioned to Mary-Kate. She smiled down at Lisa, pleased to note she was sleeping. Hurrying across the large floor, she joined Dane.

"Mary-Kate, Mike's been hurt," he told her.

"Oh, no." She turned and looked at Lisa, then back at Dane.

"I don't want Lisa to know. I'm going to have her on the first lift out, and I want you to go with her. We'll see to Mike, and when we know how things are going with her we'll tell him. But someone needs to go with her." His eyes stared down into hers, and softened.

"You don't have to wait for the supply boat after all; you can get off the island today," he said softly, his arms coming around her.

"But..." Mary-Kate didn't say anything, just hugged him tightly. She'd go. She'd known she had to go all along. "Take care," she whispered, afraid to look at him for fear he'd see her secret written on her face.

"You too." He kissed her cheek, and let her go. He was gone before she reached Lisa.

Mary-Kate was numb to the rest of the day. She climbed into the big medic-evac helicopter and sat beside Lisa, making up a story about Mike's being at the helm of the launch and joining his wife as soon as the last survivors were off the ship.

The coast guard medic gave Lisa a sedative, and she soon fell asleep. The others for the trip were belted in, and the helicopter lifted away from the island, dancing and swirling around in the buffeting wind, heading for Honolulu.

Mary-Kate tried to take a last look at the island, but the rain blurred against the windows and made visibility impossible. She sighed, holding Lisa's hand, wishing it were Dane's. There was a lot she could have said, should have said. Now she had left. There was no reason to return, ever.

"Goodbye, my love," she whispered, tears welling in her eyes.

CHAPTER ELEVEN

MARY-KATE lay back against the pillows, tears seeping from behind her closed lids. Again. She'd already cried twice since checking into her room after leaving Lisa at Honolulu's Queens Hospital. It wouldn't do any good. Tears wouldn't ease the ache in her heart.

Her Hawaiian escapade was over. Tomorrow she was going home. She'd tried to contact the Lombards through Mr. Lombard's office. His manager had been quick to offer to pay all expenses for Mary-Kate's return home, and a bonus as compensation for the misadventure. The money was wired immediately to her hotel. The yacht had already started for Los Angeles, and did not wish to return for Mary-Kate because of the stormy weather.

She had started to express incredulity that they could have left her so cavalierly, but held her tongue. The Lombards were as they were. And to them money could buy almost anything.

She'd called her parents, explaining her adventures, and asking them to meet her when she landed. Now she only had to find the energy to go out and get the clothes she needed for her journey home.

Lisa was doing well. Mary-Kate had checked up on her just a few minutes ago. Lisa had also talked to Mike, and was reassured that his injuries were not cause for alarm. Mike had reported the situation on the island to her, and she had relayed it to Mary-Kate. The coast guard had arrived, the Japanese ship put under tow, and all the injured evacuated.

Mary-Kate promised to stop and see Lisa before she left tomorrow.

Now the rest of the day remained. Tomorrow she'd board the plane and head for the mainland. She had declined her parents' offer to stay with them for a couple of weeks, and decided to go straight home. It would be easier to put her life back together if she was in her own place. No use postponing it by stopping off at her parents'.

Her tears ran again. She missed Dane terribly. Kept fantasizing on ways to meet him again, have him declare it all a misunderstanding. Have him declare his love for her. Wishful thinking.

She dwelt on their last evening together, in the small heaven of the plane. She wished the Japanese ship had never been near Manahakaloi. Although she told herself she couldn't miss what she'd never had, she wasn't convinced. She loved Dane Carmichael, and it would be a long time before she got over him. If she ever did. She had no pictures of him, but her memory of him was burned into her mind and her heart. Would time and years fade the memory? Would she look back when she was old, and not remember what he looked like, the strong emotion she felt for him?

She didn't think it likely.

The phone beside the bed rang. The ticket agent confirming her flight tomorrow? Mary-Kate sat up and took a deep breath. Hoping her voice didn't sound as if she'd been crying, she answered.

"I had the devil's worst time finding you!" Dane's voice growled in her ear, loud and clear and angry.

Mary-Kate swallowed; his voice sounded so dear to her. "Hi," she said at last. "I stayed with Lisa until the doctor said she was out of danger."

"I know. I talked with Lisa already, and Mike. He's doing okay. Will be up and about soon. Lisa thought you were staying at the Iliki. Are you coming back to the island?"

"No, no, I won't be coming back. I need to get home." Her voice was soft, and she hoped she kept the sadness from it.

There was a long sigh at the other end. "When are you going?"

"There's a flight out tomorrow; I called for reservations, and they're to call back to confirm. I talked to the Lombards, or rather their manager. They're paying all expenses."

It was so inconsequential. She would much rather talk about him, what he was doing, if he really missed her. But it was safer to talk about the Lombards.

"The least they could do. Where's the yacht?"

"On the way back to Los Angeles."

"Are you okay?" Was that concern in his voice?

"I'm fine. How are things on the island? Is the ship all right? Was anyone else hurt?"

"The coast guard has the ship under tow, the wind's died down, and the rain is just a drizzle now. Jim was injured with Mike; everyone else is fine. Mary-Kate, I'll come over and see you to your plane."

"There's no need, Dane. I can manage. Thanks for everything."

"I'll pick you up tomorrow morning. You'll be on the one o'clock flight, I assume?"

"Yes."

"I'll get you at eleven."

"But——"

"Good night, Mary-Kate." The connection was broken.

Mary-Kate slowly replaced the receiver, torn between wanting to see him one more time and the fresh heartache she would find on seeing him once more.

But really she was glad he was coming. They would take the last few minutes together, say goodbye better than they had on the island. The thought of his visit galvanized her into action. She would buy the prettiest thing she could find, put on makeup, and look as nice as she could for her grand farewell. He didn't want her, but maybe he could be just a little sorry she was leaving.

Promptly at eleven the next morning Dane called from the lobby. Everything she'd purchased fitted into the soft-sided case, which Mary-Kate picked up. Glancing once more around the room, she went to catch her plane.

She was looking her best. Her hair had been washed and dried, curling softly around her face. She'd used makeup sparingly, but highlighter and mascara to best advantage. Her eyes sparkled, looked large on her face. Her tan was almost uniform, and the light blue scooped-neck dress showed her figure to its best effect.

She saw him as soon as she stepped from the lift. Wearing tan trousers, a navy jacket and a crisp white shirt, Dane was standing near the door, watching the elevators. When he saw her he made no move, just watched as she walked toward him.

Pinning a bright smile on her face, Mary-Kate raised her head, walking proudly to him. Not for anything in this world would she let him know how tenuous her control was.

"You didn't have to do this," she said as she drew near.

He shrugged. "Wanted to." He brought one hand from behind his back; on his fingers dangled the bright pink bikini. "You forgot something."

She smiled and took the skimpy swimsuit, shoving it into her bag. "I won't need it in Iowa. I couldn't wear it there."

"That's too bad—you look great in it. You ready?"

She nodded, putting on the sunglasses she'd bought at long last. Smiling at his compliment, she turned to leave the hotel. Memories crowded her mind—the first time she'd worn the swimsuit, and the last. She took a deep breath—time enough for memories later. She still had to get to the plane without breaking down.

He had rented a late-model Chevrolet, its comfort in sharp contrast to the jeep. Quickly he pulled out into traffic, heading for Honolulu International Airport.

"So you didn't want the two weeks," he remarked softly.

Mary-Kate closed her eyes. Why was he making it so hard for her? Two weeks would buy her nothing but more heartache. "No. It's better if I go home now."

"Better for whom?" He reached out and took her hand, threading his fingers through hers, resting their linked hands on his hard thigh.

She swallowed and looked over at him.

"What are you doing? For the entire time I was on the island, you made it perfectly clear you didn't want me there. Now I've left and you want me back? I don't get it."

"A thank you for your help—the day camp made a big hit."

"You can get someone else for that. I have to get home."

"Did you dislike it so much?" he asked.

"No. I enjoyed my stay."

"But there's not enough to do."

"You put the words there, not me, Dane. If I had stayed, I had plenty to do with the day camp. If I lived there, I'd find plenty to do. Your house could stand some improvement. I could teach the kids, help at the office, learn lots about growing and marketing pineapple." She sighed, tugged her hand, trying to free it. He wouldn't release it. "But I don't live there, I live in Iowa, and I have plenty to do there, too."

"What, that can't wait two weeks?"

Why was he making it so hard? She didn't have anything that couldn't wait two weeks. But she didn't have the two weeks to give him. It was difficult leaving now, without making a complete fool of herself; she'd never be able to do so if she stayed another two weeks. Especially the way she thought the two weeks would go.

She didn't answer, only gazed unseeingly out the window.

They were silent for the rest of the journey. When they reached the airport, Dane parked the car, then sat for a moment, looking out the front.

"In Hawaii, aloha means hello and goodbye. I brought you a lei." He released her fingers and reached in the back, drawing out a plastic bag with a delicate ivory ginger lei. Taking it from the bag, he looped it over her head. "Aloha, Mary-Kate."

Mary-Kate drank in the fragrance of the sweet ginger, tears stinging her eyes. It reminded her of the fragrance that had wafted in her room on Manahakaloi.

"Thank you. I've never had one before." She touched the soft petals of the fragile plant, afraid to look at Dane.

His fingers reached beneath her chin, tilting her head to his satisfaction; then he leaned over and kissed her lips.

Mary-Kate pulled back. "I have to go. Thanks for seeing me to the airport." She opened the door and climbed out. Without a look behind her, she walked to the terminal, head held high, her steps firm and determined.

The airport was different from others she had been in. For one thing, there were few walls. The soft, warm breeze flowed through the building, caressing her skin, soothing her as she walked along to her gate. She would miss the soft, warm air of Hawaii. She refused to look behind her, refused to even think, lest everything be lost and she give way.

She passed through security, close to her gate now. In only a few more minutes they'd call her flight and she would be on her way back to Iowa. Her island paradise left behind. Her dream vacation in tatters.

The gate was enclosed by thick glass, to keep the noise of the jets from deafening the passengers. She stood beside one of the large glass windows, the sight of airplanes landing and departing blurred by the tears that filled her eyes. Thankful for the dark glasses, she stood as if she watched the activity on the runways. One tear trembled down, slipped beneath the glasses and trailed down her cheek.

A warm finger brushed it away.

"I hope the tears are for me," Dane said softly.

Mary-Kate looked up in surprise. He reached out and removed her glasses, staring down into her shimmery eyes.

"You can't have love without trust," Dane's voice murmured in her ear. She tried to see him clearly through the tears. "So I'm going to trust my instincts this time, and put trust where I thought I never would again. Mary-Kate, don't leave. Stay with me."

"What?"

"Stay with me. Don't go back to Iowa; come with me to Manahakaloi. Stay with me two weeks, or two years, or two lifetimes!" His hands held her arms, massaging the soft flesh, and his eyes stared intensely into hers.

"Dane?"

"I love you, Mary-Kate. I'm hoping you can say you could grow to love me."

She shook her head. "Not possible..."

His face fell, but still he held on to her as if he couldn't let go. "I thought——"

"I couldn't grow to love you, Dane. I already do."

His eyes lightened to silver, as his lips softened. "I ought to wring your neck. I almost died then."

"I almost died leaving," she said, moving closer, putting her arms around him and tilting her head back to see him, blinking to clear the tears. "Are you sure?" she asked, afraid of the answer, afraid the moment would vanish and she would be alone before the glass.

He stared down at the eyes so full of love for him, and his lips moved to claim hers as he drew her tight against his hard body, crushing the lei, its fragrance enveloping them. Mary-Kate relaxed against him, giving herself up to the pleasure his touch always brought.

"Two weeks?" she murmured provocatively against his mouth.

He pulled back marginally, slanting a disturbing glance down at her. "Actually, I really want the two lifetimes—yours and mine. Will you marry me, Mary-Kate?"

She was shocked; from thinking she would never see him again to a proposal of marriage in only three minutes was startling. Startling and wonderful. Nodding her head, she reached up to kiss him again.

"Then maybe we don't need to stay here?" He glanced around at the interested gazes of the other passengers.

Mary-Kate looked too, and blushed. "Let's go," she said, taking back the sunglasses and putting them firmly in place.

Reaching the car, she slid over to the middle of the seat, right up against him. As he drove back toward the town, he kissed her wrist and held her hand against his leg. Mary-Kate had trouble breathing, trouble even believing they were together; was she still at the hotel, dreaming? It seemed real, but she still wanted some things cleared up.

"Why did you change your mind? I thought you felt I wouldn't suit."

"I thought all schoolteachers wouldn't suit. I've had three different ones, all ending up the same way. My experience among other women isn't too promising, either. Look at my mother."

"But..."

"But you were different. I really thought at first that you had deliberately arranged to be left behind, and I was determined to punish you for that plan. Once I believed you had been left accidentally, I convinced myself you were like the other schoolteachers: only wanting a free meal ticket, and a chance at a glamorous life-style."

"And what finally showed you I loved you?"

"Nothing. I was taking a risk when I confessed back there. I had no indication that you felt like that about me. But when I saw you walking away, walking out of my life, I knew I couldn't let you go. I had to try, risk everything. I did know you weren't indifferent to me, from the way you responded every time I touched you."

Mary-Kate shifted self-consciously on the seat. "I can't help that. I seem to lose control when you touch me."

"I'm not complaining, sweetheart—far from that. But I thought it was just a physical reaction. And that led me to hope you could love me in time. All I wanted was time."

"And I fell in love with you from the first. I thought you looked like a pirate, but you opened your house to me. We'd get along, and then I'd say something that would make you angry and you'd back away. It was awful. I only wanted you to like me."

"And every time you made a comment on boredom, or lack of something to do, I'd hear my mother, or Melissa, or one of the school-teachers, and it reinforced my opinion of women. Your comments about Lisa and Joyce made me think, though. As did a lot of your comments."

"What if you hadn't found my hotel? What if I'd left?" Mary-Kate said in a scared voice. It seemed such a close call.

"Well, then I would have flown to Ames, Iowa, and gone to every school in town until I found you. This saved time, but the outcome would have been the same. How soon do you want to get married?"

"As soon as you want. But I want my family there."

"Of course you do. I want my father and brother. We'll call them all, and see how soon they can meet us here in Honololu. In the meantime I need to get back to the island, and make sure everything is back in order. We didn't have time for much damage assessment before I left. We'll get to work there, and fly back here when everyone else arrives. How's that?"

"I'm to go with you?" she asked, wanting it perfectly clear.

"Absolutely, darling; I'm not deserting you on another Hawaiian island—no telling who you might meet up with!"

Mary-Kate laughed softly at his teasing, resting her head on his shoulder. Happiness blossomed within her. She had her pirate, and he was taking her to his island paradise.

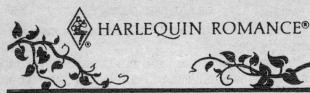

HARLEQUIN ROMANCE®

**Harlequin Romance
knows love can be dangerous!**

Don't miss
TO LOVE AND PROTECT (#3223)
by Kate Denton,
the October title in

THE BRIDAL COLLECTION

THE GROOM'S life was in peril.
THE BRIDE was hired to help him.
BUT THEIR WEDDING was *more* than
a business arrangement!

Available this month in
The Bridal Collection
JACK OF HEARTS (#3218)
by Heather Allison
Wherever Harlequin books are sold.

WED-6

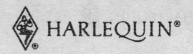
HARLEQUIN®

THE TAGGARTS OF TEXAS!

Harlequin's Ruth Jean Dale brings you
THE TAGGARTS OF TEXAS!

Those Taggart men—strong, sexy and hard to resist...

You've met Jesse James Taggart in FIREWORKS!
Harlequin Romance #3205 (July 1992)

Now meet Trey Smith—he's THE RED-BLOODED YANKEE!
Harlequin Temptation #413 (October 1992)

Then there's Daniel Boone Taggart in SHOWDOWN!
Harlequin Romance #3242 (January 1993)

And finally the Taggarts who started it all—in LEGEND!
Harlequin Historical #168 (April 1993)

Read all the Taggart romances!
Meet all the Taggart men!

Available wherever Harlequin books are sold.
